Crowds on the pier at Stornoway wave farewell to those on board
SS *Metagama* in April 1923, setting sail for Canada.

"Murray is brilliant on the push and pull of the islands on those who left … [the novel] is tender, wise and beautiful." —Antonia Senior, *The Times*, Book of the Month

"Moving, convincing and crafted with great skill … and distinguished by emotional sincerity. There is also an admirable economy … [It is written] with such skill and empathy that the novel seems to have been remembered rather than invented … arguably his best novel yet." —*The Scotsman*

"A powerful and poignant exploration of the Hebridean migrant experience." —Alastair Mabbott, *The Herald*

Praise for *As the Women Lay Dreaming*

WINNER: PAUL TORDAY MEMORIAL PRIZE 2020

SHORTLISTED: AUTHOR'S CLUB BEST FIRST NOVEL AWARD 2019 *and* HERALD SCOTTISH CULTURE LITERATURE AWARD 2019

LONGLISTED: HIGHLAND BOOK PRIZE 2018 *and* HISTORICAL WRITERS' ASSOCATION DEBUT CROWN 2019

WALTER SCOTT PRIZE "ACADEMY RECOMMENDS" LISTED

"A powerful novel … A poignant exploration of love, loss and survivor's guilt." —*Sunday Times*

"A book that's big with beauty, poetry, and heart … A wonderful achievement, a brilliant blend of fact and fiction, full of memorable images and singing lines of prose." —Sarah Waters

"A searing, poetic meditation on stoicism and loss." —Mariella Frostrup, BBC Radio 4 *Open Book*

"A classic *bildungsroman* … A work of imagination which reads like experienced truth. It's the kind of book … that can enrich your life." —Allan Massie, *The Scotsman*, Best books of 2018

"An evocative painter of landscapes and a deeply sympathetic writer … a space for forgotten voices to sound." —*Daily Mail*

"An assured journey through trauma, love and loss." —*Herald*

"I loved this book." —Douglas Stuart, Booker Prize–winning author of *Shuggie Bain*

The Salt and
the Flame

Donald S Murray

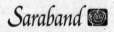
Saraband

Published by Saraband
3 Clairmont Gardens
Glasgow, G3 7LW

ISBN: 9781915089892
eISBN: 9781916812024

10 9 8 7 6 5 4 3 2

Printed and bound in Great Britain by Clays Ltd, Elcograf SpA.

In memory of my neighbour
Angus Graham / Aonghas Shuathain (1900–1992),
who, when I was a child sometimes told me
stories about his years in Ontario.

To Iain Gordon Macdonald for his
customary kindness and assistance.

Also to Magnus Graham and Liza Mulholland, who
accompanied me on a visit to Ontario, Chicago and Detroit.
This book would not have been possible without them.

To Calum Alex MacMillan, Willie Campbell,
Doug Robertson, Steve Bull, Christine and Mireille Hanson,
Charlie McKerron, Liza Mulholland (again!) and the
wonderful Dolina MacLennan, who were my companions
in the production 'In the Wake of Metagama', from
Stornoway to Barra (and Inverness) in 2023.

To Maggie – as usual – for all her love and support.

'We cannot escape our origins, however hard we try, those origins which contain the key – could we but find it – to all that we later become.'

Notes of a Native Son, *James Baldwin*

Comharra Stuiridh

Siud an t-eilean às an t-sealladh
mar a shiùbhlas am bàta,
mar a chunnaic iomadh bàrd e
eadar liunn is iargan,
's fir eile a bha 'n teanga fo fiacaill,
's deòir a' dalladh –
dùbhradh neo-dearbh is uinneagan a' fannadh.

Landmark

There goes the island out of sight
as the boat sails on,
as seen by many a bard
through sorrow and beer
and by others, tongue under tooth
and tears blinding
an ill-defined shadow and windows fading.

Dòmhnall Macamhlaigh / Donald Macaulay (1930–2017)

One

When Mairead set out on the SS *Metagama* that day, it was Reverend MacQueen's sermon a few Sundays before that kept swirling through her mind. He had drawn his inspiration from the Book of Genesis, how Sodom and Gomorrah had been destroyed after the Lord had threatened to 'rain fire out of heaven' on the two cities, destroying the people who lived there for their sins.

'"Do not look back on these places," God had told Lot, one of the few God-fearing men who lived there. "If you do, you will be destroyed too."' MacQueen looked down from his pulpit, taking in every face of the congregation that had gathered within the walls of the church in the village of Cross, noting their expressions of doubt and certainty; how sometimes their eyes journeyed round the other people in the community, observing the changes that had taken place in one another over the years. 'And so, Lot repeated the news he had been given to his family, his wife, sons-in-law and daughters. "Escape for thy life; look not behind thee, neither stay thou in all the plain, escape to the mountain, lest thou be consumed."'

He paused then, his wrinkled fingers flexing before resting on the pulpit edge, his thick grey eyebrows and blue eyes becoming more intense as he looked up and down the church once more.

'Yet some of them did not listen to Lot's advice. Instead, his sons-in-law rejected his words, mocking all he said. His wife, well, she listened – but only in the beginning. Together with their daughters, she ran away from the city alongside him, but then she heard the explosions, the walls tumbling down, and then she made her mistake. She glanced back at the place she had left, thinking, perhaps, of her old home and whether it was still upright. Or it might have been her old friends and neighbours, relatives and others that she knew. And then what happened? As the smoke of the country went up as the smoke of a furnace, she looked back then behind Lot and she became a pillar of salt, punished for her indecision, for her longing to return to that city which had been destroyed by God.'

A further pause. A moment of breathlessness as MacQueen turned silent, allowing those in the congregation to create images in their own mind of the destruction of a city. The sky burning, orange, vile and poisonous. People's lungs and faces coated with dust and soot. Spurts of blood everywhere. Buildings falling and crumbling. Rats and humans racing left and right, unsure of where to go.

For some in the congregation, imagining these scenes was all too easy. Mairead's brother, Murdo, sat nearby. He had fought in the Battle of the Somme. He had seen buildings blaze and smoulder during his time in uniform, heard the rattle of gunfire, the screams and shouts of men and women racing to escape all that was happening around them.

He was not alone in this. Mairead could see many other men sitting in the pews who had witnessed the world being destroyed around them, women who had suffered the consequences of that ruin and annihilation on those with whom they shared their lives. It was not only the Great War, the fighting in the Dardanelles or naval or merchant ships sunk in the Atlantic or the North Sea. Sometimes it was closer to home than that. Those like Mairead's neighbour Tormod, who had survived the sinking of the *Iolaire* near Stornoway harbour a few months after the war was over. Perhaps they shivered in a different way than the minister had intended when he began his service that day. Memories being whisked up and swirled. Nightmares re-awakened. Salt streaking cheeks as tears flooded down the face of a woman from Swainbost.

'God asks us not to look back sometimes. He did that too when Moses took the children of Israel to the Promised Land, rejecting their pleas to return to Egypt when that journey became hard and difficult. The same might be true of those among you who are heading off to North America, whether Canada or the States, in the weeks to come. He told Moses that they had no choice but to go forwards. "Why do you seek the living among the dead?" Carry on, the Lord informed them. Don't turn your heads and gaze back where you've been. Move forwards instead. Sometimes it is the only place where redemption and relief can be found.'

Mairead nodded inwardly, agreeing with all the minister had said that day, now recalling his words just as she was set to board the *Metagama* for Montreal. Many of the rest of the people she saw around her were clutching their loved ones even as they moved away, struggling to release them. She left her own parents near the gate of Martin's Memorial Church, not far from where a woman and a young, fair-headed man with a cloth cap were holding and kissing one another, as if they were terrified of taking one more step towards the harbour.

'I'll do my best to be patient,' she heard the woman say.

'Good.'

Mairead was the opposite. She took a long hard look at her father and mother, her brother Murdo, too, who had all travelled more than twenty miles with her from their home village of South Dell to the town of Stornoway.

'Don't come down to the harbour with me,' she said, repeating words she'd declared before they left home. 'It'll be hard enough to walk down that street, without watching you by my side. And I don't want any long hugs either. Just a quick hold. I want to stay upright all the way down to the *Metagama*. Not feel my legs rocking below me as I go on my way.'

'You sure?' Her father looked betrayed and annoyed by her words. 'I know you said that earlier but—'

'Yes, yes,' she said before her face started to flush. 'Of course I'm not sure. But I have to pretend. You can see that. Can't you? Can't you?'

Her mouth gushed and trembled as she spoke, choking on the words. She watched her brother Murdo nod in agreement with her.

'I can understand that. I felt the same way the day I went off to the war. I didn't want to see any of you around me.'

'That was different,' her father declared. 'There were lots of other young men from the district with you. Plenty of company for you to keep. Mairead's different. As a woman, she'll be almost alone.'

'Aye. But there's more than a few similarities too. She'll be thinking the same things that were on my mind.'

She nodded in agreement. 'That's what's in my head,' she said. 'I might just crumble if I lift my head and see you standing on the pier. I don't want to look back. Only forwards.'

'To the doctor's house?' her mother muttered.

'Yes,' she said, recalling the job she would have when she arrived in Toronto, looking after Dr Jardine's three children. 'That's what I'm keeping in my head.'

'I suppose you have to,' her father admitted finally. 'Stop yourself looking back.'

'Yes. Yes. I've no other choice but to do that.'

'Aye,' her mother agreed, 'we all have to do what we can to get by.'

Mairead looked down the length of Francis Street again, seeing some of the people there. One man, who was clearly not travelling on the *Metagama*, had a coil of rope looped around his shoulder; long enough, perhaps, to fasten and tie the vessel in the harbour from which it was due to sail. A woman was near the town hall. Trembling and tearful, she was being consoled by others, their fingers clasped around her back, tapping her shoulders again and again. It was the kind of scene she did not want her own family to indulge in, fearing that if they did, she might want to turn back to a village in which she could see no glimpse of the future, locked away in the past. 'Tsk, tsk,' she heard one of her comforters say. 'He'll be back some day. I'm sure of that.' And the woman responding by saying, 'My son! My son! There's no chance of that ever happening. No chance at all.'

Mairead pretended not to hear her, not wanting to think of returning to South Dell, not even to see the cairn some of her fellow emigrants had added stones to on the shoreline of Loch Sgriachabhat the night before. This had been first created by people who'd left the island before, heading to the Eastern Townships in Quebec near the end of the previous century. She had been told, too, that a few of the men had also built a bonfire high upon the shoreline, a long way from the beach at the mouth of the river on the northern edge of the community; doing this in the hope that those leaving would catch a small reminder of their homeland when the *Metagama* sailed past.

'If the weather's good, you'll probably see it when the ship sails round the Butt of Lewis. A faint memory of home.'

Again, Mairead shook her head when she heard this. She had decided that the moment she stepped on board, she would not look back at the island again, avoiding even glimpsing its coastline if she could. Even if her head did turn accidentally, she was certain the sights she had mentioned would be clouded in a thousand different ways. The glow and flame of a bonfire would be obscured by rain or mist or the salt of tears that would always be in danger of blurring her vision. The cairn of stones rendered invisible by the wings and plumage of the seabirds that had discovered it beside the loch, perching there as if each ledge was a bough or branch. Gulls would sit perched on its crest; small birds – like sparrows and starlings – landing on its layers. Perhaps, too, the terns nesting round nearby Loch Drollabhat would rise up, obscuring the coast with the swiftness of their flight.

It didn't matter. She tried to shake all thought of the place from her head. MacQueen had been right that day in the pulpit. It wasn't healthy to look back.

She kept all this tight within her head as she looked towards her parents one last time, taking in their every gesture and feature as if she feared it might slip from her in a short time. There was her father's gaunt face, his skin ravaged by so many years working on moor and shore, the spit of rain that so often lashed his features when he laboured on his croft. Her mother was different, her hair still dark with only a glimmer or two of grey, her face soft and well-rounded, quivering as she sought to suppress the sadness that she felt. Mairead hugged them both, trying not to draw too close to them but keep a little distance away, to prevent herself from succumbing to the sadness she felt all around Stornoway that day.

And then there was her brother Murdo, his face as round as his mother's, fair head the same shade as her own, bottom lip trembling. He had spoken more to her in the last week than he had done at any time since he came back from the war, babbling for ages about the family croft.

'If you marry and have children, I'll make sure your family gets the croft,' he would say. 'They can always come back here to live if things don't work out for them away.'

'And what about you? Won't you have a family?'

He shivered the one occasion he answered that. 'No chance of that.'

'Why not?'

'The war put me off all notion of that.'

She tried to question him about this, but he never responded, shrugging and walking away from her side.

He didn't do that today. Instead, he held onto her tightly, ignoring her attempts to keep them apart. He could feel a sob ripple through his body, one that she immediately tried to stifle and suppress in her own.

'Bye,' he said. 'Just remember the croft is waiting for your children. It's theirs if they want.'

'Yes … Yes … Yes … I'll remember that.'

But she was already trying her best not to recall it, bringing all that she disliked about it to the forefront of her mind. The stink of peat within the house. The manure heap behind it. The smell of cow-dung she could frequently smell within it.

'Bye,' she said. 'Bye … Bye.'

And then she was away, straight down to Number One Quay, where the *Metagama* was waiting a short distance out of the harbour, not looking in any direction but in front of her, passing the town hall, the criss-cross of roads and streets that were barely familiar to her, since she had rarely gone to Stornoway before. A short time later, she joined the queue for the filling of forms, her medical inspection; her eyes clamped, too, on the back of the head of Finlay, a Ness man a few years older than her sixteen years of age. He stood just before her. She noted his wave of black hair, the slimness of his frame, ignoring the words of other Lewismen who stood behind and in front of her, aware that, with the advent of nerves and fears at the prospect of the voyage, she might be unable to speak to them, her knowledge of both Gaelic and English slipping from mind and tongue.

Two

Finlay kept an eye on Mairead for much of the day, watching the way she stood apart from most of the others on the deck, even the woman Ina from South Lochs with whom, together with two girls who had sailed from Fife, she shared a cabin.

He even noticed that she stayed still when the pipe band played near the shoreline, just responding with a brisk nod of the head when one of the town's Girl Guides handed her a Bible. It was only when they started to sing that he noticed any reaction, her lips blurring as she sounded out the words.

> 'S e Dia as tèarmann dhuinn gu beachd,
> ar spionnadh e 's ar treis:
> An aimsir carraid agus teinn,
> ar cobhair e ro-dheas.

> Mar sin ged ghluaist' an talamh trom,
> chan adhbhar eagail dhuinn:
> Ged thilgeadh fòs na slèibhtean mòr
> am buillsgean fairg' is tuinn.

> God is our refuge and our strength,
> in straits a present aid;
> Therefore, although the earth remove,
> we will not be afraid:

> Though hills amidst the seas be cast;
> though waters roaring make,
> and troubled be; yea, though the hills,
> by swelling seas do shake.

She hadn't always been quiet like that. Finlay had spoken to her a few times when they'd been at church in Cross together, occupying a nearby seat with her parents and brother. She had been friendly then, smiling as she went past, recognising him from their days in school together. He came from the village of Swainbost, a few miles away from her home, the second youngest in a family of seven, with four older brothers and two sisters. He had also spent much of his time with his father's cousins Murdo and Tormod, who worked as blacksmiths in South Dell, learning all the skills that these older men possessed, feeling safer a distance away from the family house – a place where there were continual quarrels and squabbles. Two or three years older than her, as she was only around sixteen years of age, he had been aware of her even then – her fair hair often dishevelled and disarrayed by the wind, her face sometimes flushed and reddened by either the wind or her own embarrassment, blue eyes that could play host to a rather puzzled expression. There had been a similar look on her face today, such as when, as one of the few women on board, she had been given a bouquet of flowers by one of the town councillors.

'From the Lews Castle Gardens,' the man declared. 'Courtesy of Lord Leverhulme.'

Despite the way men cheered when she was handed this, Mairead shook a little. Like so many others from the island, she had a faint mistrust of Lord Leverhulme. He was one of the reasons why some of those on the ship, especially from the country areas, were leaving the island. Many in rural parts had signed up for the Great War after being promised they would receive land if they did so. With all his talk of the fishing industry and the benefits it would bring to the island, Leverhulme had gone back on this, wanting instead to cling on to every acre of land that was part of a farm in places like Galson and Gress, seeing in their wide stretch of acres a means by which communities like those in Stornoway and Carloway might be fed. One of their family's close neighbours, Angus Morrison, would sneer each time their landlord's name was mentioned.

'What else would you expect from a damn soap man? Nothing but froth and bubble.'

And then there was the sense that Lord Leverhulme was investing in a false dream, that the fishing industry had come to an end in these parts. Before the war, German and Russian boats used to anchor round the island's coastline. Now they were gone. The Germans too poor to trade; the Russian state in chaos. Everywhere people looked, there was bleakness and shadows. The future dull and dim. It was this that brought men like Finlay on board the *Metagama*. The legacy of the war. Empty pockets. Even how the crops had failed in the district of Ness over the last couple of years. The prospect that – unlike his eldest brother Alasdair – he had no chance of ever gaining the family croft. There was even the sense that their old lives were over, that there was a new mechanical way of looking at the world, that engines and machinery were the future, the plough and the pitchfork part of the past. The way grief, too, shadowed them, a burden stacked upon their backs.

It was as if Mairead was all too aware of this, one reason why she stood aloof from the rest of them. It came to Finlay's mind that she might be right doing this, guarding herself from the sense of loss and desolation that affected so many on the boat. Leaving her homeland because some doctor from Toronto had hired her to look after his family, she wasn't like most of the men on board. Many of them had signed an agreement to travel to the province of Manitoba, to work on a farm there.

Their ability to wield a spade and scythe would be valuable in the acres that stretched out beyond the horizon there.

'Not that I'm going to stay that long,' Donald, one of the men he had met that day, admitted. 'I'll be leaving before the next harvest if I can.'

'I'm the same,' Finlay confessed. 'As soon as I can stuff a few dollars in my pocket, I'll be on my way. There's a lot to learn if we're going to cope with all that's going to happen in the years ahead.'

'Aye.'

He looked across at Mairead, wondering if she could be persuaded to come along with him in a year or so's time, when, perhaps, the doctor no longer needed a Gaelic-speaking woman – like his wife from Golspie – to look after their children. There was something about her that reminded him of the shoreline of his native village – her blue eyes reminiscent of the sea on a fine day, the shade of her hair recalling the sand on the beach, the roundness of her face. It was all so unlike him, with his thick black hair and tawny skin, jutting nose and jaw, the height that sometimes taunted the fierceness of the wind. He hoped that she might root him, give him the opportunity to belong to the new land to which they were bound.

But, somehow, the direction of her gaze kept casting doubt on that thought. Her eyes kept wandering in towards those on the *Metagama* who were not from the island, as if her curiosity about the world outside the islands was defining the way she looked not only at the ship but the world that lay beyond it. She watched a black man with a mop wiping clean the deck. A Chinese man who worked in one of the kitchens, scurrying back and forth with a box of potatoes in his hands. Even a few men from elsewhere who looked awkward among the islanders, having had to journey quite a distance north to catch the liner. One of them clasped rotary beads in his fingers, mumbling a prayer when the psalm echoed across the harbour, as if his own words in honour of the Virgin Mary were some form of protection from the Presbyterian voices he was hearing all around him.

And then there were the Fifers, the men from the Salvation Army who had joined them on board, the Jews whose prayers had also echoed over the seafront earlier that day, fleeing the death and destruction that had been visited on their people somewhere in Eastern Europe.

'*Baruch atah Adonai, Eloheinu Melech ha'olam, hamotzi lechem min ha'aretz.*' (Blessed are you, Lord our God, King of the universe, who brings forth bread from the earth.)

'They're quite different from us,' Donald had said earlier. 'We're just emigrants, leaving our homes for a better life. They're here to make sure they have some kind of life at all.'

'How do you know that?' Finlay asked.

'One of the sailors – a Gaelic speaker from Cape Breton – told me. He'd met this fellow from a town called Ovruch. He'd fled the place after this army arrived. Their leader brought out all the Jews and told them, "I know you are Bolshveiks, and that all your kin are Bolshveiks and that all the Yids are Bolshveiks. Take them to the synagogue and I will slaughter them there." It was after that some of these poor people fled the country, with some of them arriving in Latvia where they caught the *Metagama* to sail west. They didn't feel safe in Eastern Europe anymore.'

Finlay trembled when he heard this, aware that some of his fellow passengers came from a darker, deadlier location than he could ever imagine. It was this that prompted him to slip below and look at how the steamship worked, what the engineers and others were doing down there, that legacy of his time watching the cousins, the blacksmiths in South Dell, still part of the way he thought and worked. Another place of peace – just like the forge in Mairead's home village had been when his father and older brother Alasdair spat at each other in rage in his family home from time to time. It was this sense of calm, too, that prompted him to walk away from where the other men gathered and towards Mairead. He half-wanted to let her know about the people she was watching there; half-wished, too, to protect her from that knowledge.

'You all right?' he asked.

She seemed startled when she turned to look at him, taking a long time to speak. 'Yes. I just don't want to look in the direction of home. I'm frightened I might break down if I do.'

'It'll be hard to avoid looking at the island.'

'I'm going to try. That's why I'm trying to stay away from most people I know. Just in case they start talking about home.'

'Even those from your home district, Ness?'

She shivered. 'Yes. Even from Ness.' She paused before she spoke once more. 'You see, I think I'm letting down my brother by leaving him in the house. The day might soon come when he's going to be forced to look after my mother and father. They're both getting on. And with the war and everything, he's been through enough already. Too many fears and terrors. I don't know how he'll cope.'

'He will. I have no doubt about that.'

'I hope so. It's going to be hard.'

They paused for a moment, their conversation interrupted by a sudden shudder passing through the ship. The *Metagama* was moving now, the long dark liner inching its way out of the harbour, the final farewells taking place. Mairead could hear people bellowing.

'Best of luck in the Promised Land!'

'Don't worry! We'll be joining you over there in a while! Look out for us!'

'Take care! *Thoir an aire!*'

Mairead could see a few people she recognised on board. There was the young, fair-headed man with the cloth cap she had seen near the gateway to Martin's Memorial Church, a young woman in his arms. He looked anxious and agitated, strolling up and down the deck, examining the sheer variety of people that were crowded there. Sometimes, too, he even bumped into others, as if he was unable to cope with how many he was seeing. There was another young man who was muttering to himself in Gaelic, weighing up the syllables of the language as if he was terrified that they might slip forever from his tongue.

'Don't worry,' she heard someone say to him. 'There's plenty of Gaels in Canada. All the way from Cape Breton and Prince Edward Island to Vancouver. Lots of people from these islands have gone in this direction before us. You'll hear their voices there.'

Finlay grinned as he listened to this also. 'You won't have to worry about that,' he declared. 'You'll be staying in a house where the woman speaks Gaelic.'

She nodded. 'I know that. In some ways, that's what worries me. I'll be in a halfway house between the old world and the new. Both looking forwards and looking back. And I'm not sure I want to look back. It's not that healthy a thing to do.'

Finlay shook his head. 'It's not always true,' he said. 'Sometimes you have to look back before you can truly look forwards. It's the only way you can be really sure of what direction you're really going in.'

'Perhaps ...'

But as the *Metagama* headed out into the Minch that April afternoon, he kept watching her, noting how she stayed rigidly in place, looking out past the peninsula of Point, the lighthouse at Tiumpan Head. He trembled a little as he looked at her, aware that there would be much else in the coming months and years that was odd and unfamiliar to them both, as different in their own way as these strange voices and accents they heard echoing round the boat. He only stopped looking in her direction when Allan, another passenger, came round, proffering a quarter-bottle of whisky he had somehow managed to smuggle on board, slipping it into his case.

'Fancy a swig of this?'

'Aye.' Finlay put it to his lips, hoping its taste would numb him, stilling some of the thoughts that were creating such turmoil in his head.

Three

It was late when Murdo reached home that night.

He helped his mother and father off the cart, aware that they were sore and tired after the length of their journey. He was only glad that no rain had fallen, though it had looked likely for a time, the clouds adding to the oppressive, cloistering feeling that was all around them, as if there was no escape from the sense of loss that crowded their thoughts. They looked older than they had seemed even the day before, the moment that they had watched Mairead walking down Francis Street stretching like eternity in their minds.

'You all right?' they kept asking one another. 'You all right?'

Silence was the only response, their heads bowed as they walked through the door of their thatched cottage. They were greeted there by Auntie Joan, Murdo's mother's sister. She had made sure their home was warm when they arrived, that a plate of soup and some fish and potatoes were waiting for them, just to make sure that neither chill nor hunger were added to the loneliness they felt on their return.

'O, mo ghràdh,' she kept saying to each one of them from time to time. 'I can't imagine how you're feeling. It must have been awful to go through that.'

Murdo nodded when she turned to him, shuffling his feet awkwardly below the table. He looked, too, at his parents' faces for their reactions. Their lips moved as if they wanted to say something but were unable to wrestle out the words.

'Still, perhaps she'll be back. The boats are getting faster these days. No more sails. Relying on coal and steam. Who knows what might happen over the next few years. There might be regular journeys back and forth across the Atlantic, taking people back and fore again and again.'

Again, there was silence at Joan's awkward attempts to cheer them, providing them with the false hope that Mairead might walk through the door again. They knew all too well that there was little chance of this happening.

Murdo felt a little relieved when there was the sound of someone coming through the barn door that was the entrance to the house, recognising the cough that accompanied it as belonging to one of their neighbours, Calum Morrison. Murdo even recognised the sound of his steps. Calum had been crippled as a young man, just when he was heading out to the war. One side of his body was paralysed. Day after day he used a stick to make his way across the terrain of the Ness moor, looking out for any sheep that might have been trapped there. He found it more difficult to do this at night, unable to make his way safely across the obstacles to be found on land.

'You want to come down to the shore with me?' Calum asked.

'Murdo's a little tired,' his mother answered. 'He's just been in Stornoway.'

'We're just going to light a bonfire there for those on the *Metagama*,' he continued, as if he hadn't heard her. 'Give them a last glimpse of home on their way west. They're doing this in a number of villages through the district. All the way from Knockaird south.'

'They are?'

'There's a lot of young lads on the boat. Some of them even going to stay in Montreal when they arrive, to work in a bank run by a man with Lewis connections there. It would be good to send them off properly.'

Eventually, Murdo nodded. 'Well, I need a rest,' he said, thinking of the long walk to the shore, 'but I suppose I'll go. It might be our last chance of saying goodbye.'

'Thanks for that. I couldn't manage it without you.'

'I know.' Murdo nodded once again, reaching for the lamp they used for walks outside at night. 'I'm happy to come.'

'You sure?' his mother asked as the two men set out the door, heading for the shoreline.

'Yes … Yes. Calum is right. It'll be good to send Mairead off properly.'

They stepped out, walking down to the place where the bonfire was about to be lit. As they clambered up the hill in the middle of the croft, Murdo felt his sight blurring, as if he were anticipating the tears the flames and smoke might spark within his eyes.

Four

There was much to disturb and unsettle Mairead over the next few days. There were Ina's constant conversations, her anxiety about the voyage making it impossible to keep her lips still for a moment. She even spoke about the two women from Fife with whom both of them were sharing a cabin. According to what Ina had heard, the pair were travelling to Canada to find husbands among the Scots who had settled there.

'Must be desperate,' Ina declared. 'Imagine not knowing the man you are to marry.'

'I suppose we're all in that situation in a way,' Mairead muttered.

'Och, I don't think you're like that at all,' Ina said. 'I've seen the way a certain gentleman looks at you. And the way you keep looking back.'

Mairead blushed in response to Ina's words but said nothing, knowing exactly to whom her companion was referring. She was conscious she was looking at Finlay in a new light, aware of his every movement and gesture, distracted by each word he spoke. She knew, too, she was having a similar effect on him, his gaze diverting continually in her direction, as if she was always on his mind. Still, it was best to keep her distance from women like Ina where thoughts like these were concerned. She could imagine her words rippling across the ocean, repeated again and again by Ina over the course of the voyage, the sound of her voice reaching the coastline of America long before the ship landed.

She treated this part of their endless conversations in much the same way as she tried to ignore, too, how at the start of their voyage, most of the others crammed the side of the ship just in front of Number One Quay. Those ashore had even clambered on top of the building that stood there, cheering and waving in the direction of the *Metagama*, where a small boat had brought 300 emigrants throughout the course of the day, all set for their long voyage west. It was as if they were trying to defy time and gravity by straddling its roof, not even conscious that it might crumble and collapse, only wanting to stretch out their fingers across the narrowness of the ocean that divided them from their relatives and friends, seeking to clasp and bring them homewards once again.

And then there was the moment they sailed round the Butt of Lewis, not far from home. She was conscious that there was the glow of bonfires all around the edge of the district, the people there burning driftwood, straw and peat, adding their own layers of smoke across the foot of crofts, the crops that people had planted there. Each blaze could be seen even more clearly because both land and sea were bright and luminous, lit up by a full and silver moon sparkling on still waters, waves that looked as if milk had been spilled on their crests; the gleam of the lighthouse adding its own burst of erratic light to the landscape, flickering in the direction of her home village across the waters that separated it from the Butt.

'Come out and see it,' she heard Iain from the village shout. 'It might be the last time we catch the light of home.'

But she shook her head, aware that if she went out to see it, there was the danger that she might become like some unusual version of Lot's wife, turning cold and rigid, trying her best not to flinch or shift with all the emotions that were mingling throughout mind and body, her regrets and fears, longings and hopes. She wasn't the only one who felt that way. There was a young man from the village of Bragar who reacted much as she did, turning down the suggestion of others to go out on deck.

'What do I owe that island? Nothing but poverty and hurt.'

They shuffled away when he said this; some of them admitting it was true but claiming he shouldn't have mentioned it.

'Just because we're leaving the place,' one of them said, 'doesn't mean that there won't be a large part of it forever in our bones.'

'What a grim thing to say.'

'Or in our nostrils,' the voice continued. 'The whiff of cow-shit in a barn. Damn peat-smoke.'

'That's why I asked them to burn down my house in Tolsta,' someone from that village declared. 'I wanted to see it being destroyed. Make sure there was no temptation ever to return.' He frowned for a moment. 'But they didn't do it. I kept looking out for a flame on the horizon.'

'Murdo ...'

And then, too, there were the shouts and yells Mairead heard in the middle of the night, echoing across the third-class apartment she shared with Ina. Sometimes it might be one of the Lewismen calling out, their fears and anxieties overcoming them as they lay in their bunks. It all reminded her a little of her brother, how he often used to shout in the darkness, as if he was still in the trenches at the Battle of the Somme.

'Oh God ... Oh God!'

Perhaps, among some of the older ones, it might also be a memory of their years at war, the crash of a wave bringing back the blast of a bomb or the rattle of gunfire to their heads, forcing them to recall their time in the trenches or at sea. Or it might be their fears about what lay ahead of them, their nerves and fears disturbing their slumber. Ina was the one who spoke

mainly about this. Sometimes she would even go out to iden-
tify the person who had disturbed their sleep.

'That was Neil from Laxdale,' she might say. 'He fought in
the Dardanelles.'

'Donald from Gress, that time. He was in the Royal Naval
Reserve. His ship was sunk twice.'

And then she might go on to talk about other matters. She
seemed to have an extraordinary capacity to know the family
secrets of those who were alongside them on the *Metagama*.
No matter what district of the island they came from, she knew
aspects of their history they were barely aware of themselves.

'That's Murdo there. His father was an Englishman. His
mother met the man when she was down south gutting herring in Great Yarmouth. When she came back home, she was
pregnant with a child.'

'There's Iain. He thinks his granny is his mother, his mother
is his older sister …'

'Kenny's only here because his family wanted to get rid of
him. He's too much fondness for drink.'

'You know Calum over there has plenty of Gaelic. But he
only speaks English when he talks to you. He thinks it makes
him sound a lot more intelligent and sophisticated.'

On other nights, different matters caught her attention.
They could hear even more desperate shouts echoing from
the accommodation near the stern of the liner. The rooms
there were occupied by the Jews and Poles, giving voice to the
torment they had suffered before they stepped on board. Ina
would mutter impatiently when she heard them.

'That nonsense once again,' Ina might say, clenching her
hands over her ears. 'It's like my wee sister having a nightmare.
You'd think they'd grow out of that.'

Mairead would recall overhearing one of the passengers, Donald, and his words about how their lives were so different from those they had experienced on Lewis. 'We're just emigrants, leaving our homes for a better life. They're here to make sure they have some kind of life at all. Every day their existence was at risk when they walked around the towns and villages they came from. We don't know how lucky we are compared to these people. Not at all.'

Sometimes, too, the wind and sea imitated the high-pitched screaming they heard, their lives unsettled by the coming of a storm. The liner pitched from trough to crest, unsettling many of those on board, making them long once again for the land they had left. One man, Neil from the village of Carloway, told her he had written all these letters for his girlfriend back at home.

'I put them in a pack and put dates on them, telling her what was happening in my life when I was away. Letting her know I had got a new job in Detroit at Ford's factory, helping to make Model Ts. Telling her I had moved there.'

She looked askance at the broad, burly man in front of her. 'But how do you know all this?'

'Och, I don't.' His face flushed. 'But I thought that would comfort her. I'll send her the true letters later. In these ways, I'm just making it all up.'

And then she watched George, the young man from the village of Tolsta she had first seen with the girl near Martin's Memorial Church. He had sat down with her and Ina in the ship's restaurant, clearly in distress as he picked away at his food.

'I made the wrong choice coming here,' he declared. 'I should have stayed at home with Jessie. Never made a journey this far away,'

The two women looked at one another, aware there was something disturbed about the young man. His fair hair was tousled and twisted, eyes milling over with tears. His hands wrangled one another, never staying still.

'Well, you're on your way now, whatever you think. You can send her money once you start earning a living over there,' Ina answered, the same intense expression on her face as she always possessed. There was something about her that Mairead found unusual and different. Her black hair – as intertwined as yarn for a loom, or seaweed – was as dark as what she imagined a Spaniard might possess. For all that her eyes were blue, her complexion resembled the colour of the first layer of peat cut from the bank.

'Who knows? Who knows if I'll ever be able to afford that?'

'You've got to hope you will,' Mairead said.

'If you don't have hope, you'll not be able to carry on. True of you. True of any of us,' Ina added.

'Y-yes. Yes. I know that,' he stammered.

'Well, try to keep your spirits up. It's hard enough for any of us to cope at the moment.'

He wandered off a short time later, looking anxious and agitated, crumpling pieces of paper in his hand. Mairead kept her gaze on him for a long time, aware that she might think just like him if she had looked back on the island that day, noting how it was disappearing from sight, how even the people who existed there had become blurred and indistinct as the miles stretched and grew. Despite the distance, however, a few kept looking back all the time. They would gather on the deck and teach each other songs from their home area, their voices echoing across the deck, mingling too with the tunes of a bagpipe played by a man they called Monty. She heard songs from

Harris and North Uist with which she was unfamiliar, even some from the other districts on the island. One that kept echoing were words about the Gaelic language, as if they feared that the moment they stepped on the quayside at Montreal, all knowledge of the tongue might slip from their mind and lip.

Eilean Leòdhais, Eilean Leòdhais,
Eilean Leòdhais leis a' Ghàidhlig,
An taobh an Ear tha Rubh' 'n t-Siumpain,
Seo, a rùin, san deacha m' àrach.

'S ann nam measg a rugadh òg mi,
Ann an Leòdhas a chaidh m' àrach,
Far 'n do dh'ionnsaich mi bhith 'g òran,
Measg nan òighean air an àirigh.

Isle of Lewis, Isle of Lewis,
Isle of Lewis, Gaelic speaking,
On the east side there's Rubh' 'n t-Siumpain,
Where, my love, I was brought up.

I was born among them
And in Lewis I was raised
Where I learned to compose songs
Among the maidens at the sheiling.

And then there were others who were more like her, only looking forwards and away from the lives they had existed within before – the tight clasp with which both moor and sea imposed upon the village boundaries, the clutch of the familiar, the narrowness of croft and shore circling their days. The men who gathered in the restaurant, especially in the darkness when the night had paused the passage of the ship, spoke about those who had gone away years before to Canada, the States, Australia, New Zealand, even South Africa, their voices rising and falling like the waves that washed around the boat as they talked about those who had left home and croft to travel across the world.

'There's one of our cousins in New South Wales. Surrounded by Aborigines there ...'

'There's a fellow from Ness in Rhodesia ...'

'Someone from our village has even ended up in Patagonia ...'

Mairead would half-listen to all they said, wondering about the strangeness of the existence she would come to know over the next few years and whether she was prepared for it, unsure how she might ever cope.

Five

A week or so after her departure came the moment that Murdo missed his sister most. Both he and his father had been awake for much of the previous few days, watching over the cow in the barn attached to their home, aware she was about to give birth. At just a glance, he had known his father was exhausted even before he started performing this task. He had not been himself since Mairead and a few others from the village had sailed away on the *Metagama*. He would often recite a litany of their names, shaking his head when he completed it.

'There was nothing to keep them here. Nothing.'

His sense of loss had added to the greyness of his features, the absence of his daughter making him wearier and older than he seemed before.

'You go to bed,' Murdo said at around midnight or so.

'You sure?'

'Aye, I'll manage on my own.'

'Well' – his father gave a reluctant nod of his head – 'call me if anything happens.'

'I will. You just go to bed now. You need it.'

Yet an hour or so later, Murdo also felt tired and exhausted, his eyes slamming shut from time to time as he sat perched on his stool. The cow, too, did not look as if she was about to give birth that night. There was little movement about her, all still and calm except for the constant rhythm of her jaws. Little evidence of any of the agony or strain that accompanied the arrival of a calf. Eventually, he decided it was safe to go to bed and catch up on his sleep.

A short time after wrapping himself in his blanket, the

lowing began. He turned over, barely aware of the sound, going to sleep once more. He woke up again a little while afterwards, conscious that the noise was becoming greater, the call of the cow louder and louder. Looking up at the clock in the glow of the peat fire, he saw it was nearly four o'clock. He had slept much longer than he'd planned. As he looked towards his parents' room, he could see or hear no movement, the door fully closed. Perhaps it was due to the emotional exhaustion they had suffered over the last while that there was nothing stirring. Perhaps, too, that was the reason he had slept so deep. Lifting the lamp in his fingers, he went out to see how the poor beast was. The distress evident in her moaning gave him a message about that before he even stepped out the door.

The cow's head was wedged into a corner of her stall, haunches trembling as pain rippled through her, her legs stretched as far as possible. He could see the calf too – or at least most of the creature. Its head was not much distance away from the floor of the barn, one of its back legs still trapped within the mother. He could even see its tongue, still and drooping from its mouth as if it were making some kind of attempt to stretch to the ground below. It was clear at a glance that the calf was dead, and it might not be too long before its mother followed her.

'Dad!' he yelled, knowing he needed help. It was the first time he had been in a situation like this, and he needed someone at least to point the way, to show him how he should react. His father had probably known moments like this in the past, where the life of a cow was threatened giving birth. That wasn't true of Murdo – one of the few benefits of having been away at war for four years.

'Dad!' he shouted again.

When there was no response, he tried another tack, one that faltered almost as soon as the words left his lips.

'Mairead! Mairead!'

He suddenly realised she wasn't there anymore, that he might have to go to his neighbours – Tormod, his wife Catriona, brother Calum – and wake them up, but even that wasn't possible. It would take far too long. There was no choice but to do it on his own. He stretched out his fingers towards the calf, finding it soaked in its own birthing fluid. He cursed himself for how deeply he'd slept. Clearly the calf had been hanging there for ages.

'Dad!' he yelled again, desperate to avoid performing the task on his own.

Yet there was no choice. He heaved his fingers deep into the cow, trying to find a way to tuck his hand around the leg that was still trapped there. No response. His grip failed him. He shoved his shoulder against the calf's head and tried once more to shift it. This time there was movement. The cow responded to his efforts with a sudden bawl, expressing the agony she felt. He pushed himself once more against the creature's flank, trying to free the calf's corpse.

'Good girl,' he said to the cow. 'Good girl.'

Almost as he said this, he felt his shoulders flinch once more. The words were those he had heard a thousand times from his parents, directing them either at Mairead or his older sister, Murdina, before she had died.

'Good girl. Good girl.'

He moaned as the calf slid to the floor, landing in the straw that lay there, its passage eased by the mix of fluid and afterbirth that accompanied her. The cow moved away, kicking out her hooves, lowing once again, clearly relieved that she had somehow escaped her long confinement.

Murdo felt himself bite back tears as he watched her. Not just for the calf that had been lost, the suffering its mother had gone through, but because he had also somehow caught a glimpse of his own future, the days ahead when he would be without his own mother and father, caught forever in the coldness and isolation of his home.

Six

Once she came to know her, Ina reminded Mairead a little of Lot's wife. Sitting at the table or inside their compartment, she would be constantly talking about her relatives and neighbours back home, telling stories about all they had done in their lives, their quirks and eccentricities, ways of expressing themselves, the twists and turns they had experienced in their lifetimes.

'My aunt was a herring girl. I remember when I was young, the way she would tell us about how much she hated going from port to port down the east coast. One minute, she was in Wick. The next, Aberdeen or Whitby. Finally, she ended up in Great Yarmouth. It wasn't long before she found a husband and a home there. "Saves me travelling from place to place," she told me. "I won't be moving from there ever again. No indeed."' Ina sipped her cup of tea before she spoke again. 'Well, I won't be like that. If there's ever a chance I can go home again, I'll take it. Even if it's only for a wee while.'

And: 'Katie, who lives near us, goes out for a fag behind the house all the time. One of the few women in the place who does that. Every time there's fog or heavy cloud over the village, my uncle Donald says, "Oh, that must be Katie heading for a smoke once again. She's responsible for every layer of mist that ever clouds the district."'

Once she even spoke about how quickly her father could dig when he was out working in the peats, talking about how well he could wield his spade. 'One minute there's a wee hole. A notch in the turf. Two minutes later and it's the size of a creel. Enough to bury a sheep. The next thing and you could drop a dead cow in there. A huge, huge hole. I don't think there's the like of him anywhere in the island. Like the whirl of the wind when he's got a spade attached. A blade in constant motion.'

But George was even worse. When he was not being sick like many of the others, racing to the side of the boat each time there was a squall, he seemed to spend most of the voyage regretting he had ever stepped on the liner, his condition becoming ever more apparent the closer they came to the Canadian coast. He would look at the swathes of wind and cloud on the horizon, hear rain approaching the *Metagama* from the horizon, how it hammered the ocean as if it were a herd of horses coming in their direction, striking the waves again and again with its hooves. He would sometimes stand on the deck until his skin was soaked, showers slashing through the layers of his clothes, watching one of the icebergs the vessel passed on its way.

'I should never have come here,' he would say, shivering.

'Why not?'

'There was comfort for me at home sometimes. No sign of that here.'

'You're not helping yourself,' Finlay told him one time he was in their company. 'Most people head for shelter when it's pelting down like that.'

'Not me … Not me. I feel trapped even when I'm in the ship's restaurant. All these pillars round me, waiting to topple down.'

And then came the moment the passengers were told that they would not be arriving in Montreal as they had been told.

'The harbour there is all frozen up. Skinned with ice. Impossible to get into it. We'll have to go elsewhere.'

'Where to?'

'Saint John, New Brunswick. It's on the Bay of Fundy. Ice is never a problem there.'

'Good,' Finlay said. 'We can get a train there, I hope?'

Mairead noticed that his voice lightened when he said this, aware it would be his first time seeing a train engine.

'Oh yes, that's not an issue. I'm sure they'll arrange that for you.'

'That'll be fine.'

This was not the case with George. He got worse after that, wandering around the deck for hours on end regardless of whether a storm had descended or not, both wind and wave catching him broadside as he stood looking at the horizon. Sometimes he was barely coherent, talking about how the boat stayed still at night, unable to move because of how icebergs and frozen seas stalled the vessel in darkness. Even Montreal harbour being blocked by ice was a sign that he – and others like him – were travelling in the wrong direction by going to Canada.

'I made a mistake,' he kept muttering. 'I made a mistake. And even the seas are telling me that.'

And then came the morning there was no sight of him anymore. No one knew what happened to him. Any sound he'd made had been blurred and made indistinct, perhaps, by the raucous chorus of wheeling seabirds that followed the vessel, the wind that rifled its way across the deck of the *Metagama*. The only thing that echoed was his absence the following morning, a time when they were beginning to see the occasional flash of a lighthouse, an array of sheer rocks that stood occasionally in the water, an iceberg or two. Sometimes Mairead could not help herself thinking of home when she saw them. There were puffins, gulls, birds that looked like guillemots she had glimpsed on the coastline of South Dell, though they were larger here. The thought of George diverted her from them when Finlay came to speak to her at breakfast.

'Any idea where he is?'

She shook her head and then – like Ina – went out to search for him with the others, asking the sailors if they had seen a tall, fair-haired man during the night. They all shook their heads, shrugging, then began to help them look for George. Someone suggested that perhaps he was hiding on board.

'He might be a stowaway, hoping that the *Metagama* will be going back to Stornoway, or at least Scotland, sometime soon.'

Others shook their heads.

'I doubt that. He would have no idea where this boat was going to.'

'He was so upset that I don't think that thought would have come to his head.'

'We should have been keeping a closer eye on him. He was so deluded.'

There was no doubt that he was gone, somewhere within the ocean's swell and fall, impossible to find. It would not be long before either seals or whales consumed him, the seabirds tearing out his eyes. Mairead shivered when she thought of this, how the life of one of the island's emigrants had already been lost before the ship arrived at Saint John. It never occurred to her that this might happen before the vessel had even docked.

'The poor, poor soul,' Ina kept saying. 'I would never have guessed that might happen.'

And then there was the talk that began as the ship neared the harbour, when they could glimpse some of the landmarks that were around Saint John – the Martello tower that stood on a hilltop, the wooden walls of nearby Fort Howe. There was, too, the bustle of the harbour, lights winking from various windows in the town, the ships lined up there because Montreal harbour was still crammed with layers of ice.

'They're suggesting we don't tell anyone what happened to George,' Finlay said.

'Why not?'

'It would just alarm them at home, the thought that one of their number didn't make it to harbour. We don't want them worrying about that.'

Ina nodded. 'That's probably sensible.'

Mairead thought of when she had first seen George; how he had embraced that young girl outside the gates of Martin's Memorial Church, showing his affection for her in a way she had never seen a man from the country areas of Lewis do before. He had clung to her tightly, seeking to protect her from the sadness and sorrow that was pulsing through her body, trying his best to keep her upright. Mairead shook the recollection from her head, however, trying her best once again not to look back on her past life on the island.

'All right,' she said. 'I won't say anything. I'll be like the rest of you. I'll just stay quiet.'

Yet George was in all their heads as they queued to leave the boat that afternoon, the darkness of his absence casting greater shadows than all the buildings that surrounded them on the quayside. Some of its streets were swathed with water, sparkling with the faint glow of sunshine. Finlay stood near her, talking endlessly as he did so.

'Worst rain for fifty years here, apparently,' he declared.

'I've heard that,' she said.

'The kind of greeting we'd expect.'

And then he began speaking about other matters, jabbering away endlessly.

'Apparently this is a very Loyalist place. Not like Montreal. That's full of the French.'

'Bitterly cold here. Feel like I'm still at home.'

'You wouldn't mind if I sent you a letter? It would be good to keep in touch.'

She nodded at this request, welcoming his offer. 'Yes. I'll give you my address,' she said, scribbling it down on a piece of paper.

'Thanks. Thanks. I'll treasure that.'

After that they were separated for a time, the two of them going to the immigration sheds for their medical inspection. The doctor and nurse talking about how thorough it had to be, the examination of each aspect of their body.

'There have been times in the past when passengers have brought illness and plague all the way from Europe. We must be sure you're carrying nothing like that.'

She nodded, understanding the reason they were doing this. There had been an outbreak of Spanish Flu after the war, affecting even some near her home.

'You're fine,' he pronounced. 'Welcome to the Dominion of Canada.'

His words and handshake came just before the moment she stepped upon the harbour, the cries of gulls and the sound of bagpipes played by Monty and a few others welcoming her on land once more.

Seven

After sitting for endless hours on the train, both in darkness and light, Finlay felt strange arriving at the Canadian Pacific Railway Station in Winnipeg. His legs were as solid and heavy as the pillars that surrounded the building's entrance; his eyes tired and sore, blinking continually. The only comfort was that he had not been sick like some of the others, running to the toilet and retching as if they were still on board the *Metagama*, their journey on land imitating the days and long still nights they had spent at sea. This experience had become worse the nearer they came to Canada, the water on board ship running out, leaving little left to wash away the stink and smell of vomit that some people began to trail around them everywhere they walked on deck.

And then, too, there were the experiences they had encountered when the boat had finally come to shore after eleven days steaming across the Atlantic. How their train – like the *Metagama* itself – had been delayed, this time by flooding for a day or two, forcing them to return once again to the cabins where they had slept before. They had listened to speeches of welcome, even gone to see a few films like Hall Caine's *The Christian* in the local cinema. He had sat on the opposite side of the aisle from Mairead when that had been shown, watching her movements more closely than what was occurring on the screen, the flick of her fingers through her hair, the rustle of her feet.

Despite this, there was much to divert his gaze when he finally made his journey west. There were the endless stretches of green wheatfields they passed through, the countless games of rummy he and the other men had played in their carriage. Even the city emerging from the dull, flat acres of land came as a surprise after the anonymous, indistinct nature of much of their journey, tall buildings encroaching the skyline, crammed together after so many miles of emptiness. Now there was the curve of the station's roof, the grill that resembled tiny Union Jacks on the floor above, the people, both men and women of such varied appearances, who gathered round there queuing for the train, the constant presence of clocks on walls, even the occasional gust of steam. He brushed his fingers against the station wall as he walked along the way, admiring the cream-coloured shade of its stone, the dark speckles, too, to be found on its surface. It looked very different from the rocks he had been familiar with at home on the island.

'That's Tyndall Stone,' their new boss, Rendall, declared when he saw him doing this. 'It's quarried not far away for where you're going to stay.'

Rendall was among the first to choose men from among the Hebrideans and others on the Assisted Passengers scheme who had come on the train that day, selecting those whose backs and arms looked strong and firm enough to harvest the wheatfields that he owned. Rendall himself looked somewhat misshapen. While his legs and chest were slim, his stomach protruded over his waistline, barely held back by the tightness of his belt. His thin, grey face screwed up as he contemplated the men standing in front of him. He told them that all his people had come from Orkney a generation or two before, travelling to the New World as a result of his work in the Hudson's Bay Company. 'There were loads of them, along with orphans from places like Cork, Glasgow, London. They raided the places there and took hundreds with them.'

'Ever been in Orkney?' he asked the men before he started his choice.

'I have,' Kenneth from the village of Shawbost said.

'How?'

'I spent part of the war in Scapa Flow,' he said. 'Was in the Royal Navy there.'

'Oh, those skills won't come in too useful on my farm. We're much too far from the Atlantic.'

'Don't worry. I have other skills. Coming from the west side of the island, I'm even good at dealing with stone.'

'Oh, I'm sure. I'm sure.' Rendall laughed, a rare occurrence on his clenched, stern features. 'Well, I'll pick you then. At least you might be able to tell me stories about Kirkwall and Stromness.'

'Thanks.'

'My pleasure.' And then his finger stabbed in the direction of those who stood before him, choosing around a half-dozen he wanted to work on his farm. Finlay was among them, wincing as he imagined the impact of the poke upon his chest. For all his connections with the Scottish islands, it was clear Rendall had no great sentimental attachment to them. He saw them purely as a source of labour for which he could pay poorly, barking orders at them – unlike, say, those from Eastern Europe or elsewhere – in a way that they could easily understand. His existing workforce, too, would more easily understand what these new farm labourers were saying about them than if he hired his workforce from another country. 'One of them even has Gaelic,' he said. 'Someone who came from Lochgilphead twenty years ago or more. So, he'll be able to translate if anyone mutters behind our backs.'

And then he was flicking his hand once again, up and down like a blade or a set of scissors. 'Come with me,' he said. 'I've booked a table for us all at the Oxford Hotel.'

They followed him out the doorway, their legs – despite their tiredness – moving quickly and speedily. It was during that time that the wonder of the city began to have the greatest effect on Finlay. He saw the various engines all around him – vans, lorries, locomotives – and he tried to take in the intricacies of their machinery with a quick swirl of his gaze. He saw a range of banks and insurance company headquarters, the high grey towers of Wesley College and the law courts. There seemed, too, to be a huge variety of churches and other religious buildings, often close together at the corners of streets, almost as many as the languages they heard echoing around them, all coming from faces of different shades and complexions, many of which sounded like the cries of seabirds to his ears. Finlay tried to take all of this in. There were even some Japanese-looking women, which Rendall called 'picture brides', and some native people who had belonged to this part of the world for ages before white men arrived. Russian exiles, too, and a wooden synagogue with the Star of David crossing one of its windows.

'Hell,' he heard Kenneth declare, 'there's even more kirks here than in Stornoway. A Free Kirk and a Martin's Memorial Church towering over every inch of the place.'

Finlay smiled, looking at the tough, brawling figure with thick fair hair walking alongside him, his voice echoing among the tall buildings that surrounded them.

'And how many tongues and ways of speaking is God forced to listen to here? Kenneth continued. 'You'd think the Almighty was in need of a little peace. Everyone gabbling away here, all using different languages and ways of praying.'

Eventually they arrived at the Oxford Hotel, its red walls looking very unusual and different to them. It was Kenneth who rubbed his fingers up and down the stones of the building.

'All very different from what we've known,' he declared.

And then they were in the building, gathering around the tables that were set out there. Even the table spreads and cutlery felt odd and alien to them. At home, they had so often used their fingers, perched on chairs around the fireside, the smell of peat-smoke even flavouring the food they ate.

'Sorry. I know that most of you are islanders. Probably more used to fish than beef. But it's stew I ordered for you here. Hope you enjoy it.' Rendall grinned. 'But if you don't, I don't give a damn.'

'Thanks,' some of them muttered, 'we appreciate this.'

Finlay sipped the glass of bourbon he'd been given and then did something he had rarely done when he was in Ness: prayed quietly to God before beginning to eat the meal, doing this not only for himself and his family but also for Mairead, who had probably arrived at the doctor's house in Toronto by now, working there with the family's children.

She came to his mind in different ways these days. Sometimes he imagined her lying beside him in the darkness, the weight of her curved breasts on his arm, her thighs stretched out beside his own, picturing all the secrets of her naked skin. There were occasions when the train rattled, or the *Metagama* swayed, when he would wake from his sleep, picturing this, his face and body hot and sweating, hoping that no one around him would notice the discomfort he was in.

And then there were the moments when she generated a different kind of warmth in him, times like when the two of them had stepped into the telegram office in Saint John together, wanting to send a message home.

'ARRIVED SAFELY IN THE DOMINION. WILL WRITE SOON,' he had scrawled.

'IN CANADA,' she had written. 'SAFE AND WELL.'

She'd turned towards him afterwards. 'I keep thinking of George,' she said. 'Especially after writing these words. He's not alive and well.'

'I know.' Finlay nodded.

'Don't you think his family have a right to know what happened? Especially the girl I saw with him outside the church.'

He sighed, not knowing what to say. 'Perhaps. But what good would it do them?'

'I don't know.'

'Best to leave it, then. It's what the rest of us agreed on.'

'All right.' She nodded.

'We all have to take the same path about matters like that. There's no choice about it.'

'Yes. Yes. I suppose you're right.'

He held her for a moment then, not in the way he had envisaged when he had seen her in his troubled and exhausting night-time dreams, but in a kind embrace, tight around her shoulders, one that resembled how he had held onto his younger brother Iain the day they had discovered their dog had died.

'Shh, shh,' he said. 'It'll be fine.'

She'd remained in his head throughout the last part of the journey – at one moment filled with lust and longing, the next a sad yearning for a lost friend. He thought of her as he sat in the train with the others, watching yet more fields and villages – Whittier Junction, Birds Hill, Gonor, East Selkirk, Garson – going past while Rendall spoke for ages about the wonders of the world they were entering, ignoring the fact that they were working as indentured servants for some years, earning little money for themselves whilst they paid off their passage to Canada. His head swirled, and he looked outside while Rendall rambled on, telling them that not far from Tyndall, where they would leave the train, there was a huge quarry.

'Some of the rocks there are like marble. There's fossils found there. Signs of life from thousands of years ago. Long before man ever set his foot in these parts.'

'He's making me long to go there,' Kenneth muttered as they listened. 'I bet the men there get a lot more money than we're going to get indentured on his farm.'

'Probably.'

'He's giving me an excuse to sneak off sometime. Get a job there instead.'

As Kenneth said this, the train halted – not quite at their destination, but not that far away. Finlay had stood up, looking out at the two-horse town, one that made Stornoway look vast and overwhelming in comparison. The streets rough and unpaved. The cottages small, tight and lacking windows. A grubby-looking shop. A hostel for the quarry-workers. So, this was what he had sacrificed his life at home in Lewis for? At least there was sand on Swainbost beach that he could walk across, a lighthouse that gleamed on the horizon, moorlands he could cross to see the high peaks of Sutherland on the mainland. So much that he could stretch towards and grasp with his open hand.

Eight

When she was walking down the sidewalk in Dundas Street, she heard someone shout her name.

'Mairead!'

She turned to see who was calling. In the bustle of people, she could not make out who it might be. An endless array jostled around one another, trying to find their way up and down the street. All of different races and nationalities, they reminded her of one of the kaleidoscopes she had seen Dr Jardine's children playing with, a huge variety of clothes and appearances.

'Mairead!'

She tried her best to ignore the cry, seeking to reassure herself that it was not her name that was being called. There were others around who might be called the same as she was, coming from places that were full of her fellow islanders – like Ripley, not that far away, Cape Breton or even her own former home. In her bag, she had two letters that had just arrived. One was from Finlay in Manitoba; the other from some woman in North Tolsta back on the island. She wanted the peace, away from Dr Jardine and his family, to read them. Somewhere quiet she might go.

'Mairead!'

She heard the shout echo again, sure this time that it was her name and not just a coincidence or a gathering of letters that resembled it. She stood still, looking at the collection of faces until she was certain there was one she half-recognised, something about his features that reminded her of home. She took it all in – his grey temples and eyebrows, the flush upon his face, the blue shade of his eye, even his slight and gangling frame – and identified him as one of the Gillies family, who lived a few hundred yards away from her home. She knew, too, that he had been in the States since he was a young man, one of those who had built the cairn near Loch Sgriachabhat just before his boat was about to leave.

He gasped before he spoke to her, his lungs short of breath. 'I'm Gordon Gillies,' he said. 'I'm from your homeplace.'

He gabbled a bit after that, telling her that most people knew him as 'Gulliver' because of all the years he spent travelling around, both the States and elsewhere.

'My brother let me know that you had moved here. Were living in Dr Jardine's home. I've been keeping an eye on it from time to time. Not in any sneaky way, I can tell you. Just if I was passing the door. Nowadays I work for one of the greengrocers here and I'm sent out that way from time to time for deliveries. One reason why I'm constantly on the road. Up and down. Here, there and everywhere.'

He began to cough then, spitting into a handkerchief.

'Sorry about that,' he muttered when his coughing had finally stopped. 'A place called Trail that I worked at left behind its own trail on me.'

He paused then, gasping for breath.

'Sorry about that,' he apologised again. 'It's so good to see someone from home. Someone whose face I partly recognise. Would you like to come for a cup of coffee with me?'

'Well …'

'It won't take long.'

Finally, she nodded, aware that this was a man in distress, that however much she didn't want to look back at her time on the island, this was an individual who clearly needed to do so, who was desperate to have contact with someone who had just left home a short time before.

'We'll go to a place called Stendhal's,' he said. 'It's not far away and they make good coffee there. Would that be fine?'

Again she nodded.

'Good, good.'

They walked together, his pace brisk despite the way he often wheezed and panted, struggling for breath. They arrived at a small café near the corner of Mutual Street, the entire room lifted by the aroma of coffee, blue flowers perched in windows or at the centre of each table.

Within minutes he started to cough again.

'I haven't been right since I went to work up in British Columbia,' he confessed. 'I was in a smelter there. Working away with lead and zinc. Producing thousands of tons of sulphur. A smoky place, one where thick clouds covered the countryside for miles around. Some people used to smile when they spoke of this, saying that the more smoke the smelter produced, the more jobs and money it created. I must admit I wasn't so sure. It felt like one or two houses back in the village, ones which you couldn't step into without the tang of peat smoke clinging to every part of your body. Some days I felt I had never stepped outside them.'

He spluttered again, throat hacked by yet another cough.

'But South Dell was different from Trail. You could escape from the smoke there. Step outside the houses and go down to the shore or go out to the moor and there would be no sign of the smoke. Not like here, where there's factories, all these chimneys spewing out coal smoke. Lorries passing up and down the road. That's what keeps making me think I ought to get out of Canada. Go back home instead.'

'But there's no money to be made there,' Mairead said, not even mentioning how much he might have to endure on his voyage east, the bouts of sickness so many suffered and did not want to repeat in their lives.

'Aye. And no house either. I don't know what my sister would think if I decided to go home and live with her family. She always was a cantankerous soul. Someone you couldn't get a word in edgeways with.'

Mairead smiled, thinking how well that description applied to the man who on the opposite side of the table.

'Has she changed any?' he asked.

She took a while answering, conscious that she had to censor herself while speaking to people's relatives, something she had done all her life. In a small community, it didn't pay to open your mouth too wide.

'A little.'

'In what way?'

'She's quieter than she was.'

'Good, good. I might be able to go home, then. If I was sure I could get peace there. It would be healthier for me.'

Mairead said nothing for a while, watching the other people in the café. The owner was speaking French to one of his customers, his words rolling from his mouth like an undecipherable, unfathomable sea. He smiled in her direction, as if he was aware of the predicament she was in and wanted to give her a little sympathy.

'Are you sure you're not just one of these restless people?' she said finally. 'That once you go home, you might change your mind and want to come back again?'

'Oh, no, no.' He grinned. 'Once will be enough. From what I hear, some of these boats heading east from Montreal meet some rough and raging seas. You won't want to go back west after that. Never again.'

'I hope you're right,' she said, aware that much had changed in the village since he had last lived there. It was a place that had been badly affected by the war, the aftermath of the *Iolaire* disaster, the collapse of the fishing industry. It hadn't been like that when he'd left the place, as a young man. Hope had been on the horizon back then. 'I hope going back doesn't disappoint you too much.'

'It won't. It will be good to back.' He coughed once more. 'It will be good to have clean air to breathe.'

He left soon after that, a trail of coughs following him as he headed out the door. The others in the café all watched him leave, seeing how his footsteps mirrored the uproar from his throat, as if they were following much the same pattern, each echoing the other's progress through his life.

It was then she remembered the two letters she had in her possession, how much she wanted the peace to read them. Especially the one from Finlay. But it was the other she opened first, the letter she had received from the woman in Tolsta, the one that asked about what happened to George, her old boyfriend, after he arrived in Canada.

Where did he go to? Where on earth did he disappear?

Nine

It was the whisper of the scythe that Murdo loved, the swish and swirl that it made as it cut the stalks of the field of oats they planted on their croft, the grass, too, that they grew to provide hay for their animals, to feed them during the winter months. It was as if the blade was telling the earth various secrets, letting the insects and flies know of all that had happened during the year in their home. Mairead leaving to travel to Canada. The *Metagama* steaming by near the Butt. He had heard that one of the lightkeepers there, the friend and neighbour of a young man from Ness on board, had tapped a message in its direction, asking those on the ship which vessel it was as it came near.

'SS *Metagama*,' someone on the board had replied. 'And goodbye.'

And then the ship's horn had honked, a signal that the men from Knockaird had heard, lighting up their bonfire as it sounded.

'Goodbye. Goodbye. Goodbye,' they shouted as they set flame to the stack they had created.

The best aspect of working with the scythe, Murdo decided, was its hush. It was something he rarely had at home these days. His mother and father speaking continually about their aches and pains, the sense of loss they felt now that Mairead was absent. How, too, there was an absence of young people in the parish. 'There was a time when there were twelve people living in this house,' his father would say. 'Now there's only three of us.' In contrast to all these continual choruses of complaint, there was the rhythmic whisper of the blade, one that was only interrupted during the moments that he sharpened it with a stone. There was a beat and rhythm to that too, a different kind of music to the one that occurred when he was cutting through stalks and grass, but reassuring also, disturbed only by the occasional fly or bluebottle landing on his face, an intrusion he wiped away with his fingers.

He carried on, gripping the scythe's splintery hand, occasionally stopping to lift the oats he had cut and looping a couple of stalks around them, transforming them into a sheaf. There was a quietness about that too, a rhythm and comfort to the pattern of the task, one that he relished and enjoyed, the oat-seeds brushing against his fingers as he worked.

And then he heard the wailing in the distance, the calling out of a woman in distress. He looked up to see someone walking in the direction of his neighbours Tormod and Catriona. Her hair was wild and dishevelled, her clothes wet and stained by peat.

'Catriona!' she was calling. 'I need your help!'

He put the scythe down, walking towards the blackhouse a short distance away, wondering what had happened to the young woman. His neighbour Catriona reached the woman long before he had the chance to do so, raising up her hand to stop him coming near, aware, perhaps, of the reason for her visitor's distress.

'Shh, shh, it'll be all right.'

'I want to go down to the shore.'

'No. No. Just stay with us for a while.'

Murdo returned to his work, lifting up the scythe once more, each swirl of the blade interrupted by the sound of sobbing, which occasionally disturbed his rhythm.

He heard the story later, how this young woman, Jessie, had walked all the way across the moor from Tolsta in the hope of hearing from a man called George once more. Apparently, he had been on the *Metagama* with Mairead and had completely disappeared. She had walked to their village in the delusion that he could somehow hear her calling out his name from the coastline, her voice echoing across a multitude of waves.

'Crazy. Crazy,' Murdo's neighbour Tormod said when he spoke about her later. 'Maddened by grief. Mind you, it's not the first time something like that has happened. I've seen it too often before.'

Murdo nodded, aware that the man who lived in the nearby house had been a survivor of the *Iolaire*, the disaster that took place at the end of the Great War and killed more than 200 men.

There was more to be heard that day. When he was passing Tormod's home later that day, Catriona's loud voice echoed from the barn.

'Oh, Lord, take care of Your servant Jessie here. Teach her that there are other ways in which her words can reach the man she wishes to marry, who lives so far away from here now in the New World, where he stays. Teach her to speak instead to You so that Thou might listen, pass on the hopes and dreams, the urgency and desperation of her prayers, to the one she loves. Let us hope that, if he is so disposed, he might listen and return here to these shores or – if not – send her the means to make her own way across the seas to America. And if not, if there is no future for her and this man, teach her to be content with this, to accept the wisdom of Thy will, in the hope and trust she can find peace and contentment.'

Murdo sat down after that, writing a letter to his sister in Toronto, letting her know of all that had occurred that day; asking her, too, if she knew about the disappearance of George, what might have happened to him.

Ten

There was something about the work that reminded Finlay of being on Swainbost beach. The golden shade of the field spread all around them. The sunlight. The way, too, the rig Rendall used to harvest wheat billowed sheaves again and again on the cropped ground before them, tugged by a horse that made Finlay remember the one they owned at home. For all that it was larger and stronger, he possessed the same light brown shade as that animal. Finlay even found himself calling the horse Lochlann – the name his father used to give to the one that grazed upon their croft – telling him occasionally to take it easy, that he was wearing them out with his speed.

'*Gabh air do shocair,*' Finlay would hiss, as if an Orcadian's horse could ever speak Gaelic.

For that was one of the differences between working on Rendall's acres and on the land at home. There was the scale of the task. The sheer pace of the job they were doing. The bull wheel rattling as it rolled and spun through the crop, cutting through the wheat, spewing out sheaves that it was their task to collect and gather. Both he and Kenneth would race along beside it, bringing together eight sheaves and placing them in stooks, carefully balancing them on the ground. Unlike their lives back on Lewis, there was no time to rest or talk, even take a short break for a smoke. No women, either, helping them in their task. The talk of others lightening the burden and struggle of their work, repeating the gossip that was echoing round the district, diverting them by mentioning all that was going on. Instead, there was Rendall keeping an eye on them, judging their performance, casting a hard, frosty look in their direction, one that reminded them of what this stretch of land would look like when winter arrived.

'You know it'll be even harder next year,' he said. 'Going to get a tractor to do this instead. I'm kind of fond of old Lochlann. That's why I've kept him on.'

Kenneth nodded when he said this. 'One good reason not to stay on here,' he whispered in Finlay's direction. 'I'm planning to sneak off to Tyndall. I hear it's not just rocks they slip into your pocket there, but a few more silver dollars than you get to jingle in your pockets here.'

'Aye. I've heard that too.' Finlay grinned. 'Though if I go, I'll be heading further south. You'll be too easily caught in the quarry.'

'Oh, I don't know. I hear they cover up for you there. Dig you a hole where you can disappear.'

Yet, despite the exhaustion they suffered, there were good parts to their lives on the farm. Rendall was sharp but never brutal. His wife, with her dusky skin and long black hair plaited down her back, was always kind and generous to them. She rarely spoke but when she did, it was sometimes in Gaelic, urging them to eat the food that was before them.

'*Siuthaidibh*,' she would say, '*Ithibh sin.*'

They were words she expressed five times a day. Each time they were fed. A breakfast when they rose. Another at eight o'clock. A packed lunch around midday. A proper dinner after they washed up in the evening. Another just before bed. And all the time, she was standing near them, making sure they ate, speaking in a few words of Gaelic.

'*Siuthaidibh.*'

'Where on earth did she get her Gaelic from?' Kenneth muttered some nights. 'She looks nothing like one of us.'

'I don't know. You can ask.'

'No. I'm not going to ask. She might be hurt or offended.'

'Well, I'm not going to do it either.'

'Why not? You've got more charm than me.'

'That's exactly why I'm not going to do it.'

They would stop talking soon after that, so tired that their eyes often closed in the middle of a phrase or sentence. Sometimes Finlay tried to stay awake and write a letter to Mairead or his family at home, answering all they had asked, telling of all that was happening in his life, but his pen or pencil would falter, slipping from his fingers. Once he even woke with ink staining his fingers, his thumbprint on the bed sheets. He scrubbed this clean early the following morning, trying to make sure that no mark was left behind.

In the night, though, it was the dark that left its bruises. He'd wake sometimes and think he was still in his home village, imagining the grains of wheat that adorned the fields around him transformed once more into the crests of waves crashing against the shoreline. At other times, it was the memory of the bull wheel that woke him, ticking like the clock that used to sit on the dresser of the kitchen of his old home, reminding him that times and hours were passing. He would wake up sweating with guilt at the thought that he had yet to respond to Mairead's letter, the one in which she had told him about the letter she had got from the woman in Tolsta, the one she had been sent because one of her neighbours in South Dell had been given her address.

What do I tell her, Finlay? Do I tell her that her boyfriend killed himself on the boat going over?

He didn't know the answer to that. Indeed, his mind clouded by tiredness, he could barely think about it. It was only on the

Sunday, when he and the others travelled to church in Selkirk, that he had time to contemplate it, the wheels of the train rolling as they made their way from Tyndall station again, heading through Whittier Junction, Birds Hill, Gonor, names that were now familiar. By his side Kenneth kept talking, pointing out once more the road to the quarry where he hoped to escape one day; noting, too, how they would never get away with this behaviour back home, travelling on a train or any form of carriage to church.

'They'd go mad if they saw us doing this,' he said. 'Though we've no choice but to go this way.'

And then they were at Knox Presbyterian Church, being greeted by some of the congregation in Gaelic, voices that told them of how they had travelled to the Dominion in earlier years, finding work there. They trembled as they listened to them. One even quoted the words of Jeremiah, telling of how he kept looking back to his homeland and wanted to return there one day.

'Weep sore for him that goeth away, for he shall return no more nor see his native country.'

It was only after the service that Finlay walked down to the train station and wrote Mairead the letter he had been meaning to send, giving thought to every word he wrote, especially all she had written about the notes that both her brother and the woman in Tolsta had sent her, asking about George who had disappeared from the *Metagama*. He shivered as he scribbled down his advice.

Tell your brother what you think might have happened, but don't tell the Tolsta woman. There are others who can do that. People who know both her and her family. They will know what to say. The safe thing to do is return her letter

with a note saying that you no longer live at this address.
It will stop her sending letters like that to you again. I hope
that makes sense. Otherwise, there will be more mail like
that coming your way. She'll keep asking you questions
again and again.

After he had finished that letter, he relaxed a little and wrote
one to his family. It began,

Some days I think I'm back in Swainbost.

Eleven

There were parts of Mrs Jardine's personality that reminded Mairead of some of the neighbours she had in South Dell. She would stand for ages behind the window of her home in Strath Avenue, watching all that was occurring outdoors, how some people moved to and fro up and down the pavement, walking to the houses where either they or their relatives lived; how some, too, how some had just bought Model T Fords or other cars from across the border in Detroit and were driving them back and forth.

'That fellow's dangerous,' she would say, commenting on the way he swerved and swivelled on the road. 'Shouldn't be allowed to travel anywhere.'

And then there was all the information she had discovered about those who had gathered round her on that quiet suburban street. She'd nod in the direction of a house they'd pass on their way into the centre of the city, telling her of the inhabitants that lived there.

'They're Swedish,' she might say. 'Descendants of people who moved here last century. They've made a great success of their lives. Poor, poor, poor when they came here but hard-working. Frank's mother is connected to one of them,' she said, referring to her husband. 'A very quiet woman. I can hardly think of a time she really spoke to me.'

She'd walk a few yards further, stepping alongside Mairead as she pushed the pram, her greying hair flitting round her face, young Laura lying wrapped up in blankets. Beside them the other two children, David and Robert, were also walking, the younger one restrained by the set of reins clutched by her mother, whose head jerked back and forth as she indicated the houses they were passing.

'They're islanders like yourself. From Skye, I think, originally. Spent some time in Prince Edward Island before moving to the city.'

'The woman there was one of the main suffragettes in the city,' she announced a moment later, her nostrils flaring with contempt. 'She's still not content. Keeps arguing that the vote should be given to black and Indian women. What nonsense!'

And on it would go. 'Mackays. My husband tells me that lot are all hooked on cocaine and morphine. It's a real problem in some places round here. One of the issues with banning alcohol. Some people will find other ways to escape.'

There were some occasions when her disdain for others travelled way beyond Strath Avenue. She would speak about locations like the Ward, Regent Park, Cabbagetown and Corktown as if they were curses lining her mouth, swilling down a cup of tea or glass of wine or water each time the words passed her lips.

'I've got a relative from Brora who lives there,' she said once. 'A crook and a thief. Quite at home among all the Irish and Mexicans and other crowds who cluster there.'

And she'd swirl her arms around to warn her of the places where she should not go, listing various locations that Mairead did not yet know.

'Don't step beyond Parliament Street, Gerrard Street, Queen Street and the Don River. The last place swirls with smoke from the factories there. You can barely breathe.'

But there were other parts of Toronto which Mairead learned to love. She'd walk with the children on the banks of the Humber River, one of three that criss-crossed the city, watching how it thundered and tumbled into Lake Ontario, much larger than the Dell River she had known near her home. She went down to it on a number of occasions, bringing the family washing to scrub within its waters. She learned how to skim stones there, a skill she taught young David, showing him how to hold one in his hand and throw it across the river's surface, disturbing the gulls that had settled there squealing and squawking, watching rings rippling across the surface before the pebble eventually disappeared into the depths. She would applaud when she accomplished this, watching a smile curve across David's face, his eyes brightening.

There was another time when life soared and fell when she was in his company – the two of them sitting together on the rollercoaster, the Flyer in Sunnyside Amusement Park. It surged and swooped, spinning round and round, shifting her entire body in a way she had never known before. Sitting there, she looked down on the merry-go-rounds and all the stalls below, the people moving back and forth below them. Some of the women had bare shoulders. Others had shorter skirts than she'd ever seen before. Occasionally she could hear a jazz trumpeter play, the music odd and alien. Sometimes, too, she could hear a parent calling out to her children, using a language she had never heard before.

She knew there was more to it even than that. Every footstep brought its own mysteries. Even the electric she switched on and off with her fingers, unfamiliar to her in her island home. Mrs Jardine told her that there was much about Toronto that was hidden and concealed. Ravines covered and disguised with soil. Valleys hidden under the weight of stone and debris. There was even a river transformed into a sewer, parts of Lake Ontario reclaimed from water and transformed into land.

Burrows, tunnels running underground. Different kinds of depths from the ones she knew about at home in the island. There, her neighbours sometimes spoke of a person's grandparents or other relatives, blaming them for the way someone behaved.

'Och, you know what that family's like. They're all the same.'

Relieved to be free of all that, Mairead hugged the boy beside her, thinking sometimes, too, of how her presence on the Flyer sparked other thoughts and memories – some daft and bizarre. She could see once again the terns plunging and plummeting near Loch Drollabhat, almost brushing the scarf she often wore while wandering around her home in Ness with their beaks and wings. She was able to recall watching gannets from the shoreline, their resilience and speed in evidence as they dived deep into the waves.

But most of all, she recalled Finlay, the way her heart beat and pounded in a similar way to how it thudded sitting on the Flyer when she saw him again and again during their voyage on the *Metagama*, her feet rocking in a way that had little to do with the stirring of the waves. There was no doubt she missed him, his face even coming to mind when she held young Laura close to her, longing for the possibility of the day when they could live and have children together, seeing their family grow in whatever community they might yet come together.

These feelings persisted even when she became annoyed with him, as she had done when she'd received a letter from him a few days before. She shook whenever she thought of his words, recalling how she'd felt when the others on board the ship had decided they would keep quiet about what had occurred to George, how they would pretend that nothing had ever taken place.

Tell your brother what you think might have happened, but don't tell the Tolsta woman. There are others who can do that. People who know both her and her family. They will know what to say.

For all that, she could not help feeling guilty each time she looked back at what had occurred that day. They should have stopped to think when they arrived in Saint John, let those back in Tolsta know that George had disappeared, sending a telegram to the post office there to pass onto his family. But they hadn't done that. Instead, they had kept it all a secret, and she felt the burden of that every day, the thought spinning in her head again like the Flyer she and the boy sat upon, watching both her past life on the island and the city of Toronto whirling again and again in her head.

Twelve

Even by October, there was an edge in Rendall's voice.

'One or twice there's been blizzards during this month. Some forty years ago the people here were driven from their homes by the harshness of the weather. Finns, I think, or Swedes. Which tells you in itself how fierce the weather was. They no longer wanted to stay in these parts after the wind and snow hit them, killed some of their family and loads of their animals. They decided to move to the city instead. Much safer there.' He sucked his pipe, blowing smoke around the room as if he was adding heat to his surroundings. 'That's why we must be careful. Make sure that everything's harvested. That the cattle are in the barn as soon as possible. The sledges are all out in place. Dogs ready to pull them. We have to make sure it's all done as quickly as we can.'

For all his tiredness, Finlay nodded. He had heard Rendall speak about the subject of snowstorms a few times before, his voice darkening as if he were issuing a threat. How some years winter could come early and stay late. How the temperature could drop quickly and suddenly. How livestock and even human beings could be lost. Shaking his head in wonder, he spoke about a Scotsman called Jackson his father had come across in a neighbouring state.

'The poor man found his cattle lying in a ten-mile stretch from northwest to southeast. Each of their collapsed bodies marking the current of the wind. A few of the cows were living – just barely – but when the poor soul got them back to the barn and thawed them out, their frozen flesh came off in chunks. The poor soul never got over it.'

1923

And then there was the year when he was a young child that one of his schoolfriends had died making her way to the local school.

'The snow arrived suddenly. No one knew it was coming. She got lost somewhere, her eyelashes frozen, unable to see her way.'

He paused, unable to finish the tale he was telling, his voice failing.

'That's why you've got to be careful when you're here in winter. Always keep one eye fixed upon the house. You've got to know in which direction you should go.'

Again, Finlay nodded, looking across at Kenneth. Rendall's words were telling him something of which he was all too aware. Both would have to wait until the coming of spring before moving south. Anything else was dangerous. It was something he tried to tell Kenneth each time they spoke together, though he was not convinced the other man was listening.

'I'm sick of working on the land,' Kenneth would say again and again. 'I sailed on the *Metagama* to get away from all of this.'

'I know. I know. I feel the same way too. But now is not the time. We have to be patient.'

And so, he continued to work at whatever tasks Rendall set him to do. Gathering potatoes. Herding cattle and bringing them to the barn to be milked. There were moments when he felt he had never left home at all, especially when a strong wind blew. He would be back in Swainbost again, feeling the strength of each gust on his face, watching the grass in the fields on which the cattle grazed whip and sway, bent by its force, and wish he were away from here, ideally near Mairead in Toronto, the words of a Gaelic song coming to his head as he strolled along.

Fàsaidh smal air òr, 's fàsaidh còinneach air an aol;
'S thèid a' ghrian a còmhdachadh le ceò is le droch thìd',
Na lusan 's bòidhch' san t-Samhradh bheir an Geamhradh gu
*   neo-bhrìgh*
Ach gaol far 'n deach a dhaingneachadh cha tèid air chall an
*   tìm.*

Gold will tarnish and lime grow dulled by moss,
the sun become overcast with mist and gale,
the summer's bloom withering or yielding to winter
but true love where it's rooted will always remain.

The music was also a way of blocking out Rendall's voice when he talked endlessly about how some of his ancestors and relatives had worked for the Hudson's Bay Company when they first came to these shores, travelling to places like the Arctic Circle or Labrador.

'You Hebrideans have got it soft here. If you think it's bitter and cold here, you should try the far north. All blizzards and icicles. There was even one who worked for the Moravian mission, trying to convert the natives in their igloos to the Christian faith. That must have been really hard work. Chilling in every way.'

There was the moment, too, he spoke about his wife's background; how she, too, had been raised on an island, even if – unlike them – it was on the edge of a lake.

'It was considered safe there. Less space for a child to wander and get lost. Fish like pickerel and trout and pike in clear waters all around them. Plenty of food for them to eat. Not unlike your crowd, I guess.'

He mentioned, too, how her grandfather had come from Lewis, that this was the reason she occasionally spoke a language some called Bungee, a mix of many different tongues. Working, too, for the Hudson's Bay Company, hunting for fur and meat, he had become involved with a Cree woman many years ago.

'It's why she has one or two words from that language of yours. She snatched one or two before he died.' He grinned. 'Just as well he passed away when she was young. I wouldn't want any more of that weird tongue of yours on her lips. *Gu leor* is quite enough.'

Finlay quizzed him about this, wondering about the origins of the Lewisman that was one of his wife's forbears.

'After a few years here, that man called Murdo decided to stay with his wife's tribe, bring up their children alongside them. That wasn't so unusual back in those days. A lot of white men married women like that. Not so much these days. Their lives weren't that different from the ones they had known at home. A little more hunting. A little less ploughing. But the natives in these parts didn't compete with one another in the way white immigrants often did. Nor were they quite so greedy. He felt as if he were back home on the island from time to time, even if they didn't use that horrendous language you speak.'

Finlay bristled when he heard him talk like that, missing the sounds of the tongue that had surrounded him at home. Nowadays there were too many languages circling him. He found himself barely understanding the way some people spoke, the rhythm and meaning of their words escaping him.

Yet there were many benefits. Such as the new skills he was acquiring while he worked on Rendall's farm, especially after the Orcadian bought a tractor to replace his ageing horse Lochlann, one he planned to use to plough and harvest the fields the following year. Finlay would slip on his moleskin trousers over the other layers he already wore, put on a heavy jacket and head out to the barn where he'd work on its engine, identifying each part, ensuring it was clear of rust or grime, making certain it was in good condition. He did the same with the threshing machine, the bull wheel of the wheat-cutter he had hated so much a few months before, removing it, slipping it back on once more, screwing it as tight as he could, warming his fingers each time they grew numb and chilled before beginning the task again. Sometimes he used the skills he had observed in his uncle, hammering iron, employing the flames of a fire to bend and shape metal.

Outside the barn door, the snowflakes fell in greater number even than the midges he had sometimes seen plaguing the moor near Swainbost, circling both the people and sheep that had the misfortune of having to gather there before being shepherded indoors. The ground becoming so covered and cloaked that, each time he stepped on it, a flurry of snow stirred up wherever the soles of his snowboots had been. The snow concealed the grim solidity of the earth under a cold and chilly carpet, an obstacle that grew higher and higher each day as if a white wall was being constructed, preventing him from contacting Mairead even by letter until winter had come to an end.

In the meantime, there was only the sheep and cattle to be fed, sledges carved from birch to be tugged and pulled, the voices of the men he worked alongside, the few words of Rendall's wife each time she put food before him in a kitchen that was lined by fur and cloth, heated by an old stove.

'Siuthaidibh. Ithibh sin.'

He would nod as he did these things, desperate for spring to arrive, when he could finally make his escape.

Thirteen

Car. Windscreen. Car. Windscreen. Car. Windscreen. Car …

There were days when Finlay felt his job resembled the relentless sweep of the scythe he had swung again and again in his family croft on Lewis, his arms in a constant circle as he installed windscreens onto every car that wheeled in his direction on the factory floor. He was part of what they called the Trim Line, and it was his task to attach the windscreen to the vehicle. Dark coils draped near him as he did so, small suction pads at their ends. He did this task as well and quickly as he could, aware always that the repetitive nature of his job resembled the work he had done since the early years of his childhood.

Swing up. Swing down. Swing up …

It was about the only thing that did. There were no voices of women he could sometimes hear upon the croft. No bird song. No salt-laden wind. No real sunlight regardless of the weather outside. All around him, instead, was the smell of his workplace. Sometimes this came from the stench of dirt and oil. At other times it came from the workforce who were all doing similar tasks to his own. Car. Axle. Car. Tailpipe. Car. Mirror. Car. Hubcap. Car. Fuel Tank. Car. Ignition … Some, like him, worked on the Trim Line. Others, the Tyre Line. Others, the Frame Line. The Motor Line. Blacks tended to work in other places, their presence concealed under the toxic clouds of the spray rooms, applying paint to make the vehicles shine. Or else they might work in the foundry, drawing buckets of molten metal and pouring the contents into castings from which parts were made; stinking of sweat as they stepped across the concrete floor, all too aware how easily they might be killed if an accident occurred.

They weren't the only ones that smelled. Some stank of tobacco; the others of booze they had swallowed the night before. Many rarely washed properly, their skin and clothes making him wince and recoil every time they stepped nearby. Even when the quitting whistle blew at the end of the day, the stench was still around them. And there was the sense that when they went home, their wives would be greeted by a punch that punctuated the rhythm of their days.

Swing up. Swing down. Swing up …

And then, too, there was the way some of the men spoke to one another. A horde of blasphemies, curses and racial slurs he would never have heard at home. 'Bloody Jock' would be aimed in his direction, often coming with the accusation that people like him ran the show in the factory. 'There's too many of you in these parts,' some Frenchman or Mexican might declare. 'They should daub the walls with some of the tartans your bloody pipe bands wear.'

There were moments when he even felt some comfort in that, when he would hear the melody or words of a Gaelic song sung or whistled in the factory.

'S iomadh rud a chunna mi
'S iomadh rud a rinn mi …

Many things I saw,
Many things I did …

He would smile wryly when he heard that, the uproar surrounding him disappearing as he focused on the tune. It made the medley of other voices he overheard in the factory disappear for a moment, allowing him to pretend he was back on the family croft and think about the simplicity of the life he had spent within its boundaries; how there were days when he only heard sounds like the sheep bleating or cattle lowing, the songs and melodies of the birds that soared around him. After a moment or two of thinking like that, he'd snap his mind back to the work he was doing.

Swing up. Swing down. Swing up …

Car. Windscreen. Car. Windscreen. Car. Windscreen. Car …

He also began thinking of the last few years and all the things he and Mairead had both done and planned to do in the future. Their time together had really started after he travelled from Winnipeg on the long train ride south. He'd feared that Rendall would send out the Mounties to catch him, arresting him, perhaps, when he arrived in the station in Toronto. It was for this reason he hadn't even let Kenneth know what he was doing, frightened his friend might let slip the fact that he was planning to leave the farm – not that he wouldn't be able to guess where he was going. 'You keep dreaming about Mairead,' he would say. 'I've even heard you shouting her name in your sleep once or twice.' It was a thought that troubled him during the long journey south, that he might somehow reveal his name and identity if he fell asleep. When he reached his destination, he moved his suitcase nervously from the carriage, fearing that a policeman would tiptoe up behind him, tapping his shoulder.

'Is your name Finlay? Have you just travelled south from Manitoba?'

These fears were increased by some of the reports people visiting the farm had read in the Canadian newspapers; how some other Hebrideans had done the same as he was doing, leaving the farms on which they were employed. One of the visitors to Rendall's farm had mentioned how some of those who had been employed on fields elsewhere had slipped away as soon as chance allowed.

'Around fifty of them have done that,' the visitor said. 'What an unreliable and unsatisfactory crowd they've proved to be. There's some people talking about launching court proceedings against them and sending them home across the Atlantic again.'

But Finlay did his best to ignore all thoughts of that. Instead, he'd concentrated on the long walk around the streets of Toronto, trying to find the place where Mairead lived; seeking, too, a cheap location where he could rest and stay for a couple of nights, listening out for accents that might indicate the speaker had some connection to home.

'You got any room on the sofa?' he practised saying.

He shook and worried all the time he was there, conscious that he could not even ask the police for directions, in case they were aware that someone was on the look-out for him.

'Are you the fellow Finlay who slipped out of Rendall's farm?'

He laughed at the way he thought back then, conscious that it was the way he came from a small place, where few secrets could be hidden, that made him presume something like that could happen. He was lucky in the city in which he arrived. There were plenty of Lewismen and women within its boundaries, walking back and forth across valleys crossed by bridges, past docks and warehouses, coalyards and garages. Occasionally he could even hear a snatch of Gaelic echoing among a multitude of other languages across ravines and within its streets and hidden lanes. It was this aspect of life there that allowed him space on a sofa where he could sleep the first few nights he was there. A day or two after his arrival, a man from a village in the district of Point met him in one of the local bars near Toronto's harbourfront, offering him a job of work too, helping out in a grocery store.

'You would do us a favour,' the man said, offering him another glass as he spoke.

It was also the way he found out where Dr Jardine and his family lived, walking in the direction of their home in Strath Avenue the first Saturday he was there. It was there he came across Mairead making her way down the sidewalk towards him, her hand clutching the fingers of Dr Jardine's son. His head reeled when he saw her. *Swing up. Swing down. Swing up* … It was as if he found it very hard to focus on the woman he had decided he had come to love.

'Finlay,' he heard her gasp.

It was clear from her reaction that she shared the sense of wonder he experienced when he saw her, their hearts beating loudly as they glanced at one another. For a moment, he thought that the heat that overwhelmed them was so great it was as if they were beside two of the bonfires they he'd seen blazing near the Butt of Lewis the time they had left the island.

'Aye. It's me,' he declared. 'I'm really glad to see you.'

'I am, too. Really … Really pleased,' she said. 'I was hoping this day would come.'

'Good. Good.'

Mairead stuttered through the rest of their conversation, suggesting they should meet in Stendhal's Café in Mutual Street in a few hours, when she would be free of both work and the child by her side.

'Would that be all right?' she asked. 'What do you think?'

He nodded. 'I'm sure I can manage that.'

'I met a man from South Dell there. It's a nice place to go.'

'All right.'

It was there, among the cluster of blue flowers and the smell of coffee, that the two of them made their plans. They decided he would travel down on the train to Windsor, slipping over the border to Detroit from there.

'I've heard there are lots of people doing that,' she said. 'As well as sneaking booze across the States from there. I've heard Mrs Jardine talk about it, how they use the Lakes, places like Belle Island and a tunnel, to cross the border. Ford and the other car manufacturers pay well there. There's lots of Scots over there that will help you when you reach there. There's a Lewis Society. A St Andrew's Hall. A few churches full of Gaelic speakers. Even a Masonic Temple, if you're desperate. A lot of Lewismen have become members of that.'

He recalled looking at her in astonishment as she spoke, seeing changes in her, wondering how much this was due to being in the company of Mrs Jardine, the doctor's wife. Or perhaps the transformation had come from walking the cobbled streets of this city with all their pitching and rolling, the size and scale of her surroundings so much greater than the small village from which she came.

'And I'll join you as soon as I can.' She smiled. 'I promise that. It might take a year or so, but they're always looking for children's nurses in Detroit. There's a place called Grosse Point there. Full of posh people. Always looking for Scottish nurses to take care of their families.'

'But what about Mrs Jardine? How would she feel about that?'

'She'll help me. I'm sure about that. I've mentioned you a few times to her. She knows how much I think of you.'

'And she'll help?'

'Yes.' Mairead blushed. 'She said she would. I trust her.'

'Th-that's good,' he stuttered. 'I never expected that.'

'She's only my employer,' she added. 'She doesn't see me as a slave.'

Finlay could barely restrain himself from holding her. The coffee cup in his fingers trembled. The table round which they sat shook. He knew part of this came from the thoughts whirling around his head, how this entire conversation had delivered so much more than he had ever dreamed and expected.

He thought about it for weeks, hearing from others how friends of theirs had slipped across the border to the States.

'Murdo travelled through to Cornwall in Ontario and then managed to sneak through to New York.'

'Calum went there on a train through the St Clair Tunnel. Managed to sneak on board.'

'Donnie pretended he was invited to a wedding. He wore all his clothes below his suit.'

His journey took him on another route, passing through towns that reminded him of some of the names he had seen on the map of the British Isles in Cross primary school, places like Aldershot and London, before he finally arrived in Windsor. Each name made him feel more dislocated and isolated than he had ever experienced before, as if he was somehow in England and not on the opposite side of the Atlantic. The endless trees added to that sensation, disorientating him continually, worlds away from the tiny treeless island he had inhabited before.

After that, he managed to slip on a boat manned by a group of exiled Scotsman on the Detroit River, slipping a few dollars into their hands before he undertook the voyage.

'Don't worry,' one of them said. 'With all the boats that are passing here, a lot carrying booze from Windsor, the chances are we'll get through.'

It was this vessel that took him to the city to the south, the opposite direction from the one black slaves had taken on their Underground Railroad the previous century, travelling north to freedom. On his first night after arriving in Detroit, he slept on a bench not far from the riverbank, curling up on its wooden surface, trying his best not to draw attention to himself for fear that a city policeman might tap him on the shoulder, asking him a question similar to the one he had dreaded to hear in Toronto.

'Are you the fellow Finlay who slipped out of Rendall's farm? Do you have your legal papers on you?'

It didn't happen. The next day he wandered around the city streets, feeling walled in by all the huge buildings, hovering around the doorway of St Andrew's Hall, where some of his fellow islesmen and women often gathered. Instead of looking at the names of streets and stores, he listened out for both accents and languages, believing that sooner or later he would overhear a way of talking he could recognise. It took a long time, much longer than he expected. He heard Irish, Italian, Greek, even a chorus of Germans who were cramming into the entrance of Jacoby's, a red-walled restaurant just around the corner from the hall where Scotsmen congregated. He stiffened when he listened to them, remembering how his own dad and others had talked about the Germans at home, recalling all they had gone through in the Great War, even the sinking of the *Iolaire* in Stornoway harbour as they brought the men home from the conflict. He wondered if, somehow, they would recognise him because of his appearance and take revenge on him for all they, too, had undergone.

And then he heard it, after he passed a line of fancily dressed women who had gathered at a street corner nearby ... a snatch of Gaelic, a phrase or two he recognised from home. His body reeling in much the same way as it had done when he'd seen Mairead once again, he walked towards the speaker, a smile restoring freshness to his face.

'Can you help me?' he asked. 'I'm from the Isle of Lewis. The Hebrides. Scotland. Can you help me?'

It was this instant that began his new existence, the one that led to his life in the car factory. All the rhythms that marked his days there.

Car. Windscreen. Car. Windscreen. Car. Windscreen. Car …

Swing up. Swing down. Swing up …

Fourteen

Mairead had felt as if the entire world whirled around her that day. It wasn't just the veil and bridal gown that Mrs Jardine had allowed her to borrow for the occasion; the colours, too, of the bridal bouquet her new employers, the Dunbar-Nelsons, had given her, with petals a deeper and wider array of shades and colours than any she had ever seen in her home island, even more varied than the trees she had seen surrounding her throughout her previous years in Toronto. Yellow. Purple. Orange. Red. A thousand different types and textures of green.

There were other ways in which it was so unlike the wedding ceremonies she had seen in her home in Lewis. There were few relatives or neighbours. Her own parents and brother were not among the guests. Neither were there many of Finlay's relatives, just a distant cousin from the village of Barvas who had moved from Ripley, further north in Ontario, to across the river in Windsor a few years before. She had recognised him immediately, his features still familiar over the generations; one of a tribe of Lewis faces that remained part of their surroundings, edging their way across the Atlantic that the *Metagama* had taken days to cross.

But there were odder and more discomfiting elements to the day than that. The green-tipped tower and red roof of the Fort Street Presbyterian Church in which they were getting married was very different to those she had seen in her early life in Lewis. The cross near the altar. The star-shaped window above where the preacher spoke in two different languages. A smattering of Gaelic in which he gave them welcome. The rest of the sermon was mainly in English, even most of the songs that resounded through the building, except for the words of Psalm 30 which the precentor, a Lewisman who now lived in Livonia on the outskirts of the city, brought to mind.

Mo ghlòir gun seinneadh dhutsa cliù,
gun idir bhith na tosd:
A Dhia mo Thighearn, bheir mi dhut
mòr-bhuidheachas am feasd.

That sing thy praise my glory may,
and never silent be.
O Lord my God, for evermore
I will give thanks to thee.

The words echoed around the ceilings etched with the patterns of flowers, the paint-tinted windows – a foreign landscape to many of those who were singing. They moved their lips, imitating the vowels and consonants they heard there. It had been Finlay's suggestion to hold the wedding there, one which she attempted to argue against when they had discussed the prospect when they sat together in St Andrew's Hall one evening.

'We have to adjust,' he said, sipping his glass of whisky. 'We have to change.' And then he smiled, talking about the sermon she had spoken of a few times since they had come together once again in Detroit. 'We can't be like Lot's wife. We have to look forwards, not back.'

She nodded, grinning at the way her own story had been used against her. He was probably right. The world around them was largely rooted in the English language. It was the tongue most of their bosses spoke, the one they heard mainly in the city's streets. There might be several Gaelic singers staying in places like the boarding house where Finlay had lived for much of the last few years, run by a woman who came from the district of Lochs on their home island, but there were relatively few elsewhere. At least compared to the sheer variety of people she had come across since arriving here. The English, Irish, Germans, Glaswegians and Dundonians who clustered on the west side. The Poles, Russians, Jews and Greeks who filled much of the east. Sometimes, too, she had glimpsed Native Americans, the ones to whom this land had once belonged. And then there were the black people she saw roaming around the city streets. Many of them looked maimed and wounded, damaged by the suffering they had gone through for generations during their lives in the South. She hadn't spoken to many, but throughout her first years in Detroit, she worked alongside a woman called Emily in the Dunbar-Nelson family home at Grosse Point. She was a housemaid and often exhausted from travelling on the streetcar to and from her squalid, cramped house in the streets of Black Bottom to provide service for the household. She prepared breakfast for the family before they came downstairs each morning. She made sure their last meal was ready before travelling home.

'Where did you come from?' Mairead asked one day as they shared a table together, looking across at Emily's tired, exhausted face while the Dunbar-Nelson's youngest child slept nearby.

'I was brought up in Alabama,' she declared. 'My folks picked cotton there.'

'And was that true of everyone who lives where you are now?'

She laughed at the question. 'No. There are others who worked in lumber camps, coal towns, tobacco plantations; places like Tennessee, western Georgia, the Florida panhandle,

Alabama, following the rail lines that took us here. They all had one thing in common. Terrible, terrible places.'

'You glad to escape, then?'

'Damn right. Damn right … Life might be hard here but it's nothing compared to what it's like in the South. Nothing at all. At least, there's a half a chance for us to dream here. No chance there.' And then she went on to speak about the many days she had spent reaping cotton, how her fingers had stretched behind branches to grasp its flowers thousands of times each day, swinging upwards and downwards to clasp them.

'Sounds like my dad with his scythe when he harvested oats,' Mairead said.

'A little, perhaps.' Emily smiled. 'But your fingers don't get cramped in quite the same way. Nor are they cut by the barbs of cockleburs.'

'No. No.' Mairead blushed. 'That's true.'

'Nor do you feel you're carrying a dead body on your back by the end of the day.'

Again, Mairead's face flushed. She giggled.

'But then, I don't have to think about these things anymore. Glad to have escaped them.'

Half-aware of all the cruelties inflicted on black people in that part of the world, Mairead decided not to ask any more questions. Instead, she spoke to Finlay one night, asking what he thought of the blacks he had come across at work.

'They're very different to the others around here,' he said. 'Best if we keep our distance from them.'

'You sure?'

'Aye. There's a reason that most of the white people around these parts do. They don't trust them much.'

Mairead wasn't so certain of that. She saw similarities in them.

Even the way people from the same parts of the Deep South had gathered in Detroit, just like her fellow Hebrideans had done, drawn there by clan and kinship. And then there was how their skin had been tarnished with both soil and sweat. That, too, was not so different from how her fellow islanders had been after they'd harvested fields of oats and potatoes, even peat from the moor. Some blacks had also walked beside horses ploughing acres of land. They had probably lifted stones to build walls they could shelter behind, fashioned roofs out of turf or thatch. She noticed, too, their love of song and music, similar to many of those who came from the islands to which they belonged. They were country people like themselves, finding it hard to adjust to a new industrial life. Only their shade of skin seemed strange and different. Some parts, too, of all they had suffered through the last few centuries. Much else seemed the same.

She decided not to say any of this. Not then and not on their wedding day. Instead, she concentrated on all the others who were around them that day. A couple from Cape Breton whom Finlay had met, who spoke a strange variety of Gaelic that seemed different and all their own – a mixture, perhaps, of the dialects of Gairloch and Skye, where they said their ancestors hailed from. There were the young men with whom he had shared boarding rooms. Many of them worked in various car factories in the city. Others were involved in the creation of buildings around Detroit, their exactness in placing ridges of stone on top of one another, a skill they had learned at home, valued once more in the creation of buildings like the Union Trust and Fisher, built within this city. Even the way they had fished while balancing on cliffs, rocks and skerries during their youth was a talent that had proved useful in their new surroundings.

'It taught us how to step out on these spires,' a man named Calum declared. 'Without slipping. No danger of a wave washing us off.'

'Aye,' another Lewisman grinned. 'And at least you get a little more than a few fish for your efforts. You're paid a reasonable wage.'

And then there were others. A few who had been with them on the *Metagama*, including a young man called Donald Macleod, who had been among those who had travelled across the sea to work for Sun Life in Montreal before changing direction and heading to Detroit, employed by the car manufacturer Chrysler there. There was, too, his friend Lachie, who arrived at the wedding reception dressed in the hat and jacket of a Canadian Mountie.

'Are you the fellow who slipped out of Rendall's farm in Manitoba?' he asked in an American accent. 'We've been looking for you a long, long time.'

Others had travelled west on different ships, such as the *Marloch* or *Canada*, which left Stornoway or other ports in the Hebrides a few months before or after they had departed. They greeted each other in Gaelic, delighted to have that language restored to their lips after a year or two of shuffling it away, pretending to have forgotten every word. They slapped each other's backs, bellowing out their greetings.

'*Ciamar a tha thu?*'

'*Tha glè mhath.*'

Mairead watched as Finlay grinned, the words echoing all around him as he sat drinking at the table, his smile bright as the Masonic badge that sparkled on the lapel of his suit. She sometimes felt as if alcohol allowed him to return to the same place he had occupied before he left that day on the *Metagama*; an islander once more, instead of someone who dwelled within a city. It was like he was back in his childhood home, laughing and talking with others. It was one of a number of reasons why he had enjoyed so much going down to the shoreline or spending time helping out Tormod, Murdo or Calum as they worked upon their anvil, hammering down metal, twisting iron into the shape of a horseshoe or the blade of a plough. For all that he had sometimes resented life in his childhood home, there was no doubt that he missed people like these occasionally, wanting to hear the volume of their voices, the phrases they might say.

'Congratulations. Hope it all goes well.'

'*Meal do naidheachd!*'

'Best of luck to the two of you.'

And that lift in mood and spirits was partly caused by those whose presence surrounded him during nights and evenings that she sometimes felt herself resenting, even though he claimed it was the best way he could obtain a little extra work and money. These were the ones he had encountered on his visits to the city's St Andrew's Hall, the Masonic Temple with its Scottish Rite Cathedral within, the Lewis Society which he had joined soon after arriving in the city; people who in their exile had come together in order to help out any of their fellow islanders who suffered loss or distress during their time there. Some of them, she was aware, were fine people; but there were those, too, with whom Finlay had spent a little too much time on the occasional night or evening.

There were other folk, too, who she had met over the last few years. The Jardine family. The Dunbar-Nelsons. The women who helped take care of other children in Grosse Pointe, with its huge houses, its wide and panoramic views over Lake St Clair and all its yachts and nearby golf courses.

Each had their own warmth and friendship. There was Ina, too, whom she had not seen since she travelled south from Toronto a few years before but who kept sending letters to her, detailing all she had heard about the other passengers who had sailed across the Atlantic on the *Metagama*, *Marloch* and *Canada*.

Murdo Morrison from Skigersta in Ness has now moved to
Seattle. He's working in a brewery there. I wonder what his
parents would think of that.

John Macaulay from Shawbost has gone to Portland,
Oregon. He's working in a store there. They say someone from
your village was working there before he was killed in the
Great War. His son was brought up by his widow in the town.

Alasdair Macleod from Achmore has got married to a
woman in Manitoba. Someone told me that his bride be-
longed to a tribe called the Cree. That will start a lot of gossip
back on the island.

She was quieter on the day of the wedding, barely saying a word. She was chief bridesmaid, standing beside Mairead in the church, sitting by her at the table when Calum, the best man, read aloud the telegrams at the reception in St Andrew's Hall that night.

"'Remember your vows … Mairead: 'I do.' Finlay: 'I do what she says.' Happy wedding day.'"

"'May you live each day like your last and live each night like your first.'"

"'Great you're getting married, Finlay. You've finally found the person you want to annoy for the rest of your life. Happy wedding day.'"

"'Wonderful that you've finally found someone who'll put up with you. Congratulations! We hope to see you back annoying us one day. Murdo, Donald, John, Calum, Joanne and Agnes.'" Some laughed loudly when these words were said, their amusement all the greater because of the alcohol that had been smuggled into the reception, courtesy, perhaps, of the likes of the east side's Purple Gang, which concealed thousands of bottles in the Mosquito Fleet that crossed the Detroit River to Belle Island and the harbourfront.

And then there were the other quieter messages; these read aloud by Kenneth, who had worked alongside Finlay in Manitoba and moved south to Toronto in the past few months, finding employment in O'Keefe's Brewery, one of many that had thrived north of the border since prohibition had been introduced in the States.

"'We wish you every happiness, trusting you will share both love and God's grace. Remember that your family in Swainbost are with you in their thoughts. Mum and Dad.'"

"'Your wedding day will come and go, but may your love forever grow.'"

It was the last one, however, that made her eyes smart and well with tears.

"'Thinking of you and wishing you all our love. Only sorry we cannot be there to see this. Too long to travel from South Dell. Congrats. Murdo and your parents.'"

Fifteen

A year later, there was another communication from home that brought tears to Mairead's eyes. Her brother Murdo wrote her a letter in which he told her that their mother had become ill and taken to her bed. A week or two later there was further correspondence, a telegram from Murdo arriving at their home.

Mam passed away, it read. *So sorry to have to tell you the news.*

She felt her mind swirl, imagining once again – as she did so often these days – her brother approaching her within the walls of their old home, speaking to her about their mother's passing, shaking continually as he passed on the news.

She could feel her absence, too, as if it was spilling over from her crofthouse, across the shoreline, past the Butt of Lewis lighthouse, across rocks and skerries, the width of the Atlantic, the coast of Canada and the United States, the Great Planes and Great Lakes, towers and skyscrapers, factories and stores, towards her home.

Sixteen

Murdo felt moved by all the kindness that had been shown to him since his mother had passed away. Some of the villagers came to his home with food they'd cooked for both him and his father, bearing their offerings in their hands.

'I thought I'd bring you some of the mutton we cooked the other day. It'll be hard for you to adjust without your mother being in the house. We know she prepared all the food for you for years.'

'I just brought some fish we've been cooking. Thought it might help you out.'

He smiled, thanking them for the support they were giving. Sometimes their offering was accompanied by kind words about his mother or, indeed, his sister Mairead, away in her new life in Detroit.

'You must be missing them both,' they might say.

'A great big gap in your life …'

Again the nod, the mutter of gratitude, the few words expressed either inside or outside the door of their house. Most of the time, however, he never thought about his own grief and sorrow. Instead, his mind would slip to his recollections of his sister and how she must feel about her loss, living across the Atlantic and with no prospect of ever coming home to see either her mother's grave. At least he could think of her lying at rest in the cemetery a few miles north of the village. For Mairead, there was no such comfort, no memory she could draw upon to provide her with peace and rest.

'Poor, poor Mairead,' he would sometimes catch himself muttering, woken up by the thought of her sorrow in the middle of the night. It made a change from the usual recollections that disturbed his dreams in the darkness, the memory of his time on the Somme, the recollection of the blast of a bomb a short distance away, the screams of the men who had sat or stood nearby him only a short time before. Nevertheless, it was just another thought that haunted him, making him shiver and call out. It was this that had always made him shy away from women, either in the village or elsewhere. He was terrified that the same thing might happen to him as had occurred to one of the men from the village of Borve whom he had served alongside. He confessed he had woken up once or twice in the middle of the night with his hands around his wife's throat, convinced she was a German soldier.

'I nearly squeezed the life out of her. Imagine that. Imagine that.'

He knew that it was this thought, too, that had affected many of the women in the district. They were all too conscious that some of the men – like Mairead's father-in-law, Finlay's dad – had been damaged by the conflict and that its shadows had never left them. The same was true in a different way of some of the women. They had known grief and sorrow at an early stage in their lives. The loss of a son. The passing of a brother. They went on to spend the rest of their existence guarding themselves against even the possibility of grief and sorrow.

There was one woman, however, who came to their door more often than any other. The same age as Mairead, Dolina lived with her mother and brother, Neil John, a half-mile from Murdo's home in the neighbouring village of North Dell. She used to often make her way across the bridge that stretched over the river dividing the two communities, carrying a bowl or pan, its contents covered by a cloth. Inside, there might be a fish or a seabird that had been caught, a rabbit trapped nearby, skinned and cooked.

'Here she comes,' the blacksmith Tormod used to say when they talked together some mornings.

'Your heart must be beating faster,' his crippled brother Calum declared one time.

'Do you not think she's trying to give you a message?' Tormod's wife Catriona stated once, a grin upon her face. 'Perhaps you should listen to her.'

Murdo never said anything in response to their words. Aware that she was a vulnerable individual, he just used to walk in her direction, accepting her gift from her hands.

'Thanks,' he would mutter. 'This is greatly appreciated.'

And she would smile and blush in response, her eyelashes fluttering like the wings of starlings and sparrows, the small birds that he often saw in the fields of oats or elsewhere on his croft.

Seventeen

Finlay was worried about more than his wife.

For all that she was his greatest concern, there were other troubles. She was the one, however, that kept distracting him. He kept noting her sadness, the way she kept sighing from time to time, her back bowed as if there were a great weight stacked upon her shoulders. There was also the way he sometimes overheard her in conversation with other women, talking to them about the loss and absence she felt in her life.

'It's the only time I've wanted to go back since I arrived here,' she would say. 'I think of Murdo and Dad a lot and wonder how they're coping. The thought I might never see them again tumbles into my mind from time to time.'

The other women nodded as they listened to her. 'I've thought the same myself now and again. You can't help looking back.'

'Even if it destroys you.'

'Aye.'

'And it might …'

They nodded again, thinking of a woman they had heard about who had travelled over on the *Marloch*. She had retreated into herself, not speaking to anyone after she had been told her brother had drowned while fishing out from Lochboisdale. There was another man whose mood had become dark and disturbed after receiving similar news from home. A churchgoer for years, he now received his sole comfort from drinking rum on one of the many boats in the Mosquito Fleet that smuggled booze across the Detroit River from Windsor. 'He had a taste for the stuff when he was in the

Navy,' one of her friends called Sandra had told her a while before. 'Now he thinks of nothing else.'

'Some people just can't cope,' another woman said, shaking her head. 'It's too big an adjustment to be made.'

'Especially when you feel you've betrayed them by not being with them when they were ill.'

Mairead sighed, knowing that this was exactly how she felt, that sense increasing when she thought of how her father and brother were coping without her, unused even to cooking their own meals.

And then they would all cheer up, looking at Finlay and Mairead's new baby, Roddy, lying in his cradle. He seemed content and quiet there, lying among blankets.

'It's good to see him,' someone said. 'A sign of life being restored. A new life beginning in these parts.'

'Concentrate on him. He'll bring you a lot of comfort in your loss.'

Mairead nodded, looking at Finlay as she did so. She was all too conscious that there was a great deal swirling round his head. He had spoken about some of these things to her, how his work in the car factory was threatened by something he called the Wall Street Crash, how businesses were closing because of some failure she did not quite comprehend among the country's banks. She would watch shadows crease his forehead as he sat down to read the *Detroit News*, noting how people were losing their jobs all over the place, both within the city and beyond.

Finlay had seen how men and their families were starting to queue for food in some of the streets that weren't that far away. Others, too, who stood in a long line of workers outside the Fort Street police station in the city, waiting to fill out applications for jobs they had little chance of obtaining.

Hunger marches existed too, led by Communist speakers and mourning those who had died as a result of starvation, and the participants were sometimes beaten up by the police or guards by those who ran the motor companies. There was plenty of evidence of want and need, men with cups of soup in their hands, thin slices of bread in their fingers. He had even told Mairead that he'd come across a man from Fife who carried a poster perched on his shoulder, bearing the words:

WORK IS WHAT I WANT AND NOT CHARITY.
WHO WILL HELP ME GET A JOB?
7 YEARS IN DETROIT. NO MONEY SENT AWAY.
I HAVE EXCELLENT REFERENCES.

Once or twice Finlay even spoke about all he had witnessed, how it made him long to return home. 'At least you don't have to beg for food or peat there. There's fish and potatoes in the place. The fire is always warm.'

He would shiver as he sat there, even if he was sitting in front of their household stove, stretching out his fingers towards the heat. For all the rages that sometimes affected his mood – the way he had inherited his father's fury about his life – he knew he was one of the luckier men from both his own community and the many others who had settled over the last few years in the city. He saw them all over the place. The Greeks, Scandinavians, Italians, Spaniards, Irish, blacks. All nursing their resentments. All living in desperation in their own communities where only their tongues echoed, where an array of similar voices could be heard. Sometimes he would hear their voices reverberate with anger, call out in distress. He'd hear the blacks, especially, talk about what Klansmen had done in the city; how they'd gathered round the home of a black doctor in Garland Street, trying to chase the family from their home, and how someone in the household had shot one of the people in the crowd that was threatening them.

'It's just not right … It's just not right,' they would say, their hands flapping in anger. 'Way back in the South, the bastards used to lynch the likes of us. Now they just fire bullets in our direction. It ain't much of a change. Ain't much of a change at all.'

And then he would hear some who shared his own shade of skin, muttering about how black people even travelled in the front seats of buses in these parts.

'It's just not right,' they would declare. 'It's just not acceptable. They should keep their distance.'

'It's silly and unimportant,' Mairead would declare when she heard people talk like that. 'These things don't matter in the slightest. Only those who are daft would say otherwise.'

Finlay would try and close himself off from them, including even Mairead, trying to react in the same way he had done when he was annoyed with the loudness of his brothers' voices as they tussled or quarrelled with each other.

'Shh,' he would say to himself. 'Stay quiet and calm. *Bi sàmhach agus stòlda.*'

However, he barely managed to convince himself, conscious that all this was beginning to happen to people he knew, some he had even come across on the deck of the *Metagama*. He would relive old conversations with them, recalling the dreams and desires they anticipated when they reached their destination.

'It's the women that are on my mind,' a young lad called Allan had declared. 'I've seen a picture of a few of them over the years. They wear fancy skirts and low-cut dresses. Not the kind of clothes you ever see a girl from Tolsta put on.'

'I'm hoping I can buy a car. There was no chance of that ever happening at home.'

'I'm looking forward to eating a few steaks over there. It'll make a great change from cormorant and salt herring,' Neil from the district of South Lochs had told him as they stood watching an iceberg. 'I've eaten too much of that in my time.'

'What's great is the thought that if I decide to travel, I won't get seasick,' a man called Calum declared. 'My stomach will be settled each time I go somewhere new.'

He had smiled back then as he listened to them, conscious even at that time there was a certain falsity at the centre of their plans and hopes. More dream than reality. More fantasy than truth. But back then he could never have anticipated the troubles that were coming, how misfortune could swathe through people's lives like either the scythe or the production line where he occasionally still worked – *Car. Windscreen. Car. Windscreen. Swing up. Swing down. Swing up* ... He now made much of his income working for some of the rich men he had come across in either the Masonic Temple or St Andrew's Hall a few years before, depending on their help and support each time he fixed the engine of their car or lorry. It was the skills he had accrued either at home, helping his relatives at their blacksmith's anvil, or in the farm in Manitoba where he had spent his first year after arriving on the *Metagama*, that came to the surface then – the experience he had gathered coming back into his existence, for all that he had believed he had cast them aside some years before. Life was a little like the work he did in the car factory. *Swing up. Swing down. Swing up.*

He wasn't the only one whose life had turned out that way. He thought of Calum, who had done what he had least wanted, returning home to the family croft. He had heard about him from the Lewis Society, the organisation that had been set up by his fellow islanders to help those among their home community who were now in distress, even paying for their funerals if help was ever needed in this. Calum had apparently approached them to obtain money for his journey home.

'I know the chances are I'll probably leave my stomach down among the waves. But I have no choice but to risk it. There's nothing here for me. Not even the chance of filling my stomach again.'

Finlay had nodded, aware there was some truth in what Calum was saying. The more he thought of it, however, the more he realised he had even fewer options than the reluctant sailor to whom he was speaking. If he returned home, there would be squabbles with his brothers about who inherited the family croft; arguments he was only too aware were going on in his absence. One man from the village had told him this, that his family had become notorious in the district for their endless quarrels and fights.

'You're well off away from them,' he had said. 'You'd turn deaf if you were ever forced to step back into the family house.'

Or they might have to share croft and land with Mairead's brother Roddy and their father. It was something which Mairead had spoken about once, only for him to stifle her words.

'No. No. We're not doing that.'

She looked back at him and their son for a moment, as if to remind him that he had not only himself to think about but the two of them.

'No. No. We'll survive. This won't last forever.'

But as the months went on, it seemed more and more likely that it might. He saw some of his fellow Hebrideans retreat from the houses for which they could no longer afford to pay their mortgage. One or two of them even moved to the edges of areas like Black Bottom or Paradise Valley, where they stayed in shacks built from wood, tin or bricks while they tried to save up money for their journey home. Sometimes Finlay had nightmares about this happening to his family: sharing tumbledown buildings with black neighbours who had just travelled from the southern end of the States a few years before, about the same time he had come on the *Metagama*. He saw his child asleep, wrapped up in – what some people called – a Hooverville blanket, the headlines of the *Detroit News* below his chin as he lay there, its front page telling of the many who were jobless in the city. Mairead was bending over him after obtaining a few scraps of stale bread from a heap that lay nearby, her fingers on his forehead as if she were trying to take his temperature, her eyes wet with tears.

'No! No! No!' he yelled. 'This can't be happening. This can't be—'

He woke up, sweating, alarming Mairead by his side.

'You all right?' she asked.

'Yes ... Yes, yes.'

He shook his head. Much as he did this, it was harder still to shake the thought from his mind. The vision remained with him for ages. He could see the battered walls, the poor blacks and others shuffling around him, feel the emptiness of his stomach as he dreamed of stumbling towards the soup kitchen that was in the area. There were times he thought that if he really stumbled, then this was the place that his family could fall into, a trap into which they all could be enclosed.

And then there was the other place in which some of his fellow islanders stayed, while they tried to gather enough cash to travel homewards again. John Morrison, an elderly night-watchman at one of the city's car factories, had told him what he was doing: opening the doors of where he worked to allow some of the Lewismen and women he knew to sleep below its roof. They lay there sprawled and stretched beside the still assembly lines. Sometimes a wheel would hang above their sleeping bodies, resembling the moon in its stillness, a shiny plate at its centre.

'They keep telling me how lucky they are to be there,' John said. 'It's better than sleeping on a bench or in a doorway. Or even that place Black Bottom they keep talking about.'

'Will you get in trouble if you're caught?' Finlay asked.

'No idea. That young fellow Donald Macleod – the one who came here from Montreal – said he'd watch my back if anything happened. But I can't be sure.'

'He's young. He might not have the power.'

'Aye. I am only too aware of that.'

'Good on you, though. Good on you. I only hope these men don't hang around there forever. They need to escape.'

'It's not the easiest of places to escape from,' Morrison said. 'I've thought of doing it myself a few times and never quite managed to go.'

Finlay nodded, understanding. For all that he had been in some ways a success here – he now had his own garage, repairing cars for businessmen who lived nearby – there was a part of him that missed his home islands very much. Peculiarly, for all their narrowness, he thought there was a freedom there he did not possess in Detroit. He could walk wherever he chose, moor, machair or shoreline, with nothing to prevent him, no walls or fences – except for the occasional stretch of bog – from stepping where he sought to place his feet. He could look out at the ocean and pretend that in all its emptiness, there were places like Newfoundland or Labrador within his gaze; perhaps he could even touch them if he raised and stretched out his hand. Even the flight of birds added to that mindset. He could watch a flock of geese making their way north or south, east or west, touching down on a loch or fields. He could see the gannets, too, flying in the direction of Sùlasgeir or Sule Stack and imagine hitching a lift on their feathers, taking a ride on their feathers to escape the croftland on which he belonged.

He wasn't able to fool himself in that way in Detroit. There were too many people around him there, the stamp of feet upon road or pavement far too loud and persistent to pretend he could escape the confines of the city. He sensed, too, their anger, particularly those who had come to this location to break free from poverty or the after-effects of generations of slavery, conscious that the fury he often heard within their voices could either snipe in his direction or bring themselves crashing down. There were also too many buildings standing in the way of his vision, lurking everywhere, limiting even the way he could examine the clouds and the wide stretch of the sky. This was especially true at night. The swirls of streetlights only gave rise to shadows; men with their collars raised as they wandered down roads that sometimes looked like rivers; the broken drainpipes of certain buildings occasionally gushing like waterfalls spilling down the face of a cliff in his native island.

The streets, too, were a tangle. Each one either named or numbered. Jay Street. Washington Boulevard. Michigan Avenue. Vernon Highway. West Jefferson. Or worse, 3rd Street, 18th Avenue, 2nd Boulevard – all as if no one thought they were fit to obtain a proper title, deserving only to be part of a list. These words circled his head as if they were spokes within the cartwheel he had seen his uncle fashion and make in his childhood, spinning round and round. It would have to roll a long way before he could escape the city's boundaries, either to the likes of Lake Superior or the stretch of the Great Plains. He had heard people talk about travelling between the city and Chicago, seeing the wide stretches of fields, the endlessly straight and concrete road, even the banks of trees with all their changing colours, orange, crimson, purple, green. Even they seemed to add to his sense of entrapment. The sweep and snarl of roots twisting below the surface of the earth. The branches poking their way in the direction of windows, the edges of roads.

In some ways, life here, too, was a maze, one in which he felt trapped. For all that the land here was vaster and more gigantic, it still seemed more encircling than the island he had left behind almost a decade before. And all the time he kept trying to avoid looking backwards – at the place that Mairead had turned away from when she was on the *Metagama* – conscious that there was no way he could return.

And then he thought of his son Roddy, how he slept in his cot beside their bed.

He had to always keep him in mind, provide the child with the means to escape the limits that had entrapped him all his life.

'*Bi sàmhach agus sòlta*,' he told himself once again. 'Be quiet and calm. It's the only way you can ever be sure that your child will break free.'

Eighteen

Dolina's behaviour had become a little more discreet over the previous few months. She would arrive in darkness, making her way to his home after walking up the length of the family croft, stepping across the river as it neared the shore. Murdo would hear a rap at the door when he might be sitting opposite his father at the fireside or in a chair at the table where they ate. He'd go out to answer it to find her standing there with a bowl in her hands.

'I thought you would like this,' she might say.

A small, slight woman, she always looked at him with her chin lifted, the bottom of her face jutting out of the scarf and black clothes she had always worn since her father died some twenty years before. She had a great deal to mourn since his loss, some people said. Ever since then, her brother's unreasonable behaviour had taken over her life. Her blue eyes looked nervous as a result of that, her wisps of grey hair trembling too.

'Thanks,' he said. 'It's greatly appreciated.'

She would nod and smile, turning on her heel and walking away from the door. Once or twice, he might have enough time to ask her a question, but she would rarely answer and even then it was likely to be with a brisk shake of her head.

'Would you want to come in?'

'Is your brother fine with your coming here?'

'Does he even know about it?'

'I make sure he's either down on the shore or out on the moor when I come down to see you,' Dolina answered one time. 'I'm very careful about that.'

'But what if someone tells him?'

'Och, no one would do that. No one likes him enough to do that.'

She walked away, a skip in her step as if she was going on a dance with him, the way he imagined his sister might when she went along some nights to a Lewis Society event or one that took place in St Andrew's Hall near the centre of Detroit. He watched Dolina, hoping for her own sake that she was right. It wasn't that long afterwards that he discovered that she wasn't.

Saturday was the day Murdo did his washing and ironing. He'd haul water from the well on his croft and boil it on his small stove, using the Persil he bought in one of the local shops to make sure the shirts that Mairead had occasionally sent him from the States were clean enough to wear for church on Sunday. It was one of the goods she obtained in the stores in that country with which she seemed a little obsessed, writing once about a conversation she had with a black woman called Emily about how they harvested the cotton the item of clothing was made from.

> *It's not like you going down the croft with a scythe*, she said. *Much harder than that. But some of the men going out in the fields gather as much as four hundred pounds in a day. Twice or even three times their weight. Yet for all their hard work, they don't get much money from it. Sometimes I can even recognise a woman who's just come from the South by the shabbiness of the clothes they're wearing. Some go around wearing flour sacks as a dress, boiling them for hours until the company's names have faded away. Not that things improve very much for them when they take what they call the Overground Railroad, cross the Ohio river and head north to cities like Chicago or Detroit. They're still poor there. Sometimes I feel sorry for them.'*

And then, too, there would be the crispness of the few dollars she would sometimes send to him.

We're not that well-off here, but I'd like to see you build a new house. When we can afford it, I'll send a little more.

He had tried to dissuade her from doing this, but she dismissed his words.

I owe you that and loads more, she wrote. *Especially with your hard work looking after our parents.*

He was ironing his trousers and shirt for the Sunday sermon that Saturday evening when there was knocking on the door. First of all, it was light and could barely be heard, but it quickly became loud and thunderous, echoing through the building's walls. He put the iron back on the stove and went to answer it. Outside the door, there was Dolina's brother, Neil John. Normally a taciturn man who kept his emotions to himself, it was clear he was unable to do this anymore. His chin shook. His white hair bristled. Even his eyelashes fluttered, though not in the way Dolina's had done when she sometimes spoke to him. It was clear even from a glance that he was struggling hard to keep his temper under control.

'I've heard that Dolina's been coming to see you,' he muttered.

'Yes. She has sometimes.'

'And she's been bringing food?'

'Yes. Now and again.'

Neil John puffed out his lips, showing his dismay. 'Well, that's got to come to an end. She has her own family to feed. Her mother and me. That's enough for anyone to look after. It isn't her job to fill the stomachs of you and your dad. Not in the slightest. That's your responsibility. Not hers.'

'I don't deny that.'

'Well, why have you been accepting food from her? Isn't that such a selfish and stupid thing to do.'

Murdo didn't answer. There were a thousand reasons why he accepted food from her hands. He could see the pleasure her offering brought to her face. It lifted some of the darkness from her expression, brought a little light into her eyes. He was also acutely aware that even the walk along the village road or shoreline provided her with an escape from the imprisonment of her family home at the back of North Dell near Dun Arnaistean. Her brother was known to be a bully, one that resented the fact that his two brothers had gone to Canada and the States, leaving him and his sister to look after his ageing mother. One reason why the entire house echoed often with cries and demands. 'Dolina! Dolina!' The shout would merge with the squawk of gulls when they visited the manure heap behind the family home, as angry and insistent as the calls of terns that sometimes resounded across the village shoreline. He was providing her with an escape from that, a relief from the tyranny she endured each day.

But he said nothing about all of that, keeping mouth and tongue firm and still.

'Well, I've told her not to give you any food anymore,' Neil John continued. 'Time for you to look after your own. It's no one's responsibility but yours.'

'That's fine,' Murdo muttered. 'That's fine.'

He stood where he was, watching Neil John whirl round on his heels and go on his journey home once again, his boots loud and echoing on the track that ran through the village towards the river. He could see, too, some of his fellow villagers watching him as he went, aware perhaps what his mission had been – to put an end to his sister's kindness. They would shake their heads about how predictable his actions had been, probably wondering why they had not occurred months before this day. Perhaps he had not known what Dolina had been doing, too obsessed with his own life and his resentment against his brothers in Vancouver and California to know what her actions were.

And then Murdo got back to his usual routine on a Saturday evening, finishing the ironing, preparing food for both that evening and the following day, sitting down to write a letter to his sister in the States. In it he would mention all the births, deaths and marriages that were connected to people in the district, including Swainbost where Finlay came from. It was their way of making sure the two of them were up to date with all that was happening near the northern edge of the island they came from.

He made sure, however, he did not mention Dolina once.

Nineteen

There was one letter Mairead obtained from her brother Murdo that she did not share with Finlay.

It was one in which he told her of all the young men who had returned to the island after travelling west – like her – to Canada and the States on boats like the *Metagama*, the *Marloch* and the *Canada*.

A lot of them kept telling me about how fed up they were of the place. Some said they sailed back home because of the Depression and how few jobs there were around these days. They were sick of having empty stomachs or having to scrounge for food. Others say they came home because of the way their bosses treated them, yelling and shouting in their direction all the time without any proper unions to protect them. Others have said they just travelled back because they missed their own people. There were too many different voices over there, too many shades of skin, too many arguments. They did not feel comfortable without hearing both speech and song they recognised.

And then there were the sentences she decided she had to hide away from him.

If you ever decide to come home, just remember that there will always be space here for you. Dad and I will make sure of that. You can build a house here on the croft. It will be a space for you and the family, especially if things don't work out between you and Finlay.

For a long time, she wondered what had caused him to write these words, wondering if her brother had heard tales about her husband's behaviour, especially about those times when he drank too much and too often. Nights and days like that happened occasionally, mainly when he was not in her company. But sometimes she had seen the dark side of his personality. It loomed over them when he spoke with others, making the same point again and again.

She remembered the day Lachie – one of the men from the district of Point in their native Lewis who had worked alongside his old friend Calum on the steel beams that circled the Fisher Building, building its walls – had spoken to him about the possibility of going home. He now worked as a Teamster, driving a truck for Food Fare, one of the firms that brought meat and vegetables into the city. Finlay would often mutter about the trade union to which Lachie belonged when his fellow islander left the house, buttoning his lip until the door slammed behind his visitor.

'He's involved with a lot of dangerous creeps there. A bunch of bloody Commies and hoodlums.' And then he would shrug. 'But what else would you expect from the district of Point? That lot always caused a lot of trouble when they were in Lewis. Nothing changed when they sailed across the Atlantic.'

This time, however, Finlay had taken a drink, one of the many that sometimes slipped down his throat when he spent an evening at St Andrew's Hall or the Masonic Temple. 'They're places where I can make valuable contacts,' he had told her more than once. 'Some offer me a little work from time to time.' She had nodded, accepting there might be some truth in his words, though she wished he spent more time with her, especially as she had Roddy to look after and was expecting another child. She wondered, too, if there were hours when he should choose to drink coffee or lemonade, like some men did, rather than resort to alcohol every time.

'Wouldn't it be a good idea to go back home? It's a safer, better place to be than here,' Lachie had said, his face flushing as it often did when he spoke. His blue eyes would twitch open and close at the same time. Sometimes, too, he would flick back the fringe of his fair hair, as if it were clouding his vision or interfering with the trail of his thoughts.

'In what way?' Finlay snarled, clearly irritated by the man's words.

'You'll have food to put on the table. People around you that you know and trust.'

'Really?'

'Really. You'll know their grandparents and their kith and kin. They won't be strangers like so many are here.'

Finlay grunted, thinking, perhaps, of his brothers. He rarely heard from them. Nor were they that close to him when he was young, their household known as a fighting, feuding family throughout the district. 'Just because they're not strangers doesn't mean you can trust them all that much.'

'They're not as bad as they can be here.'

Finlay shook his head while Mairead kept thinking of all she had seen that day from the window of her home. A knife-sharpener yelling as he pushed his screeching whetstone up the street, shouting out words in a sharp and cutting voice she could barely understand. 'Blades to whet and grind! Blades to whet and grind!' A street-peddler with his whip flicking his horse as his cart rumbled down the street. A squabble around a coal lorry some young rascal had decided to leap upon, stealing a sackful of its contents. She wouldn't have seen sights like these in her home district.

'There's still more decent people here than crooks,' Finlay

snapped. 'I've come across a lot of kindness in these parts. They're not all like the Teamsters you surround yourself with.'

Lachie ignored the last remark, knowing how his fellow islander felt about the trade union to which he belonged. 'That's because you've earned it. All the hours you've worked for others. Doing them favours here, there and everywhere. Giving much of your time away to them.'

'Isn't life like that wherever you go?'

'Perhaps. But much more so here.'

'There's another side to the story.' Finlay frowned.

'What's that?'

'What kind of future would my kids have on the island?' Finlay said.

Mairead knew he had his own vision of what that might be. He had spoken about it to her on a few occasions, indulging in a few prophecies as he talked about the uncertainty they might suffer if he ever took up her suggestion and returned home. He made endless predictions, that there might be another fleet of ships like the *Metagama*, *Marloch* and *Canada* coming to the island's shores in, say, a decade or so, and they'd take the young men away to ports other than Montreal or Saint John, New Brunswick. Perhaps this time they might be heading to Sydney, Melbourne, Auckland, Wellington, Napier. There might be a similar mix of people there as there was in Detroit, but the distance would be even greater, their chances of ever turning round and travelling homewards slighter than ever.

'There isn't even the same amount of jobs there. Nothing surrounding people but kangaroos,' Mairead recalled him declaring once.

Or else they might leave the island in different kinds of boats, the type that had taken men on board in 1914, taking them to places like the Mediterranean, the North Sea, the South Atlantic, battlefields like Gallipoli, Jutland and the Baltic Sea. Finlay often shivered when he thought of this, imagining his sons clasped up in naval uniforms, parading on the deck of a battleship. 'It's happened to too many people we know,' he had told Mairead when they had spoken about going back home a few times. 'Time to put an end to it.'

He turned towards Lachie, taking another gulp of whisky. 'Well, what's your answer, Lachie? How will the children fare back in Lewis?'

'Home is a safer place than here.'

'Not in every way,' Finlay countered. 'Not in every way.' He shrugged his shoulders. 'Remember. I don't have to lock my doors here. I can trust my neighbours to keep an eye on the house. We're good at looking after one another that way.' He paused before he spoke again. 'And I know, too, that they will keep their noses out of our doors and windows. That isn't always true back on the islands.'

And then he came out with a few words that she would recall him saying later, aware that once again he was indulging in his fondness for prophecy.

'The shadows that have gathered here since the Depression will someday lift and fade. There is a future here. Not like the islands of Scotland, which have long been trapped by their past. There is no escaping from the clouds and darkness there.'

Mairead looked at him as he spoke, aware that all times and places possessed their shadows. Sometimes they might be created by high-rise towers, like the Fisher Building on which men like Lachie and Calum had worked. Or by the mobsters or indeed management teams which surrounded men like Lachie, a threat or a curse in their every word. At other times they might be caused by cliffs and skerries, the hills that swept across much of the moor. There was no escaping them. They could occur at all times of the day and night or year, the hour of their arrival never predictable or known.

'Mind you, I can understand why I might want to go back there if I was part of a mob like the Teamsters, led by a crook like Tobin. I might just step on the nearest boat to get away from them.'

'Oh, I don't know. They're not as bad as some people think. Besides, the way our bosses uses both thugs and cops for some of their behaviour, they've little choice but to act that way.'

'You're blaming everyone but yourselves. The man's nothing but a crook.'

'No. He isn't.'

'That isn't what I hear. That they hire some of the Chicago mobsters to help them out from time to time. Some of the local bosses have been hammered now and again.'

'Sometimes the bosses are the ones who do the hammering. Even the cops help them occasionally, visit workers in their homes with batons in their grip.'

'Oh, I doubt that.'

'Doubt it all you like. There's no doubt it's true.'

Tired of the way their talk was going, Mairead stepped aside. She had heard it all too often. Instead, she went to look after Roddy in their bedroom, hearing him suddenly begin to sob and cry. In a curious way, she felt relief when he did so, anxious to break free from her husband's voice. For once, there was something welcoming in the child's tears, giving her a break from Finlay's rages.

Twenty

There were many thoughts that came into Murdo's head when he saw the young men from the village gathering round the post office during the evenings of the last days of August that year. They sheltered near its walls after they had come from working in the peats or on their crofts, leaning there as they talked to one another about places they had rarely spoken about together before. Words like France, Germany and Russia, even Hitler and Stalin, crossed their lips. They also echoed words they had sometimes heard on their father's mouths – names like Dardanelles, Somme, the *Iolaire* – which they had tried to avoid mentioning before. They spoke about how men like Tormod, Murdo's next-door neighbour, who had survived the wrecking of the *Iolaire*, were reliving their entire experience again today. Or they talked about relatives who had perished in the conflict, somewhere far away from these shores, like the Mediterranean, the coastline of South America, the North Sea or near Scapa Flow in Orkney.

When Murdo came near, they questioned him about what he had seen of the war.

'What was it like?'

'Was there anything good about it?'

He laughed at the last question, before declaring there were bright lights even in the darkness of that experience. 'You see unusual places. Cities and forests. Come across people that you never imagined coming across before.'

Dolina was a short distance away when he answered that question. Her face was a little weary and tired, still marked by the tears she had been shedding since the death of her mother in the last days of July. He had nodded in her direction when he saw her, acutely aware that it might not be that long before his household endured a similar experience. His father had been short of breath the last while, gasping continually for air in the middle of the night. It was undoubtedly, however, worse for her. She had to live alone with her brother these days, the sound of his voice echoing from the walls of their house across that part of the village, making his usual loud commands.

'Dolina! Dolina! Dolina! *Trobhad ann a seo!*'

Murdo wouldn't have to cope with any of that. Instead, his problem would be the silence. Sometimes, as he was all too aware, it would usher in the memories of the conflict he had gone through all those years before. It came back to him even today – stark memories of the Battle of the Somme. The buildings in the towns and villages that burned, their walls collapsing under the weight of flame and cloud. And all around him the screams of his fellow soldiers. Sometimes they even echoed during the times when gunfire was still and there were no blasts or explosions, coming to life once more in the troubled heads of those who had experienced their onslaught. Twenty years later, he would sometimes relive each moment. The tap of rainfall on roof and barrel reminding him of gunfire. An occasional boom of thunder or the puff of wind bringing an artillery shot to mind. It was one reason that he had never even considered marrying, the thought and memory of these moments recurring again and again, never passing from his thoughts.

He knew what to do to chase away all recollections of these moments. Sometimes he would go through the pages of the *Stornoway Gazette*. At other times, he would spend hours reading the Bible or the *Pilgrim's Progress* or one of the Robert Louis Stevenson books the family had on their shelves. Mainly, however, he would spend his time studying the letters he had received from Mairead, going over all her news, the mentions of people like Ina and Lachie, as well as all the strangers she had encountered.

According to Finlay, that fellow Lachie, from the peninsula of Point, is a red flag waver. A Eugene Debs Socialist, he calls himself, named after someone who's been dead for years. He thinks of nothing but his membership of the Teamsters Union at all times. He gives all his loyalty to that Irishman who's boss of the union. He's from a place called County Clare, not so far from Lewis as a seagull flies but miles away otherwise. Finlay keeps telling Lachie he should cross himself every time he gets up in the morning. Either that or light a candle by his bed and go down on his knees every night.

Ina should be working for the Stornoway Gazette. *She's got all the news about everyone who's left our islands over the last few years. It doesn't matter if they'd landed up in Alaska or Alberta, California or the Deep South, she knows all there is to know about them.*

Mairead might even tell him secrets that she would not reveal to anyone else, especially if they came from her home country.

I hate the way some people from the islands treat black people. It makes me hate being one of them.

But it was the evening after he first saw the young men from the village gathering around the post office that a sudden thought came to him. The time was soon coming when he would receive no letters from his sister. Nor would she receive any from him. No mail would leave Stornoway to cross the Atlantic. Instead, there would only be boats filled with young men, all repeating what he had done when he was their age, sailing east or west, north or south, to travel once again to war.

Twenty-one

Unlike Hugh, his younger brother, Roddy was fascinated with boats.

He would talk about them all the time, sharing information he had obtained from Nathan, the grandfather of his classmate Charlie. One of their neighbours, Nathan, had arrived in Detroit from Wilmington in North Carolina a decade or before. A large, soft man with a wave of crinkly grey hair, he had travelled north to work in Detroit's car factories in the twenties before deciding that a life working on the boats that sailed around the Great Lakes was a much better use of his existence.

'I learned no skills in all my life working on land,' he would declare. 'The car factory's assembly lines were like sitting behind my Granda's rocking chair, watching wheels and engines going forwards and back. No wonder the men who worked there got bored to death and unhappy. Much better being at sea. At least when the waves rocked back and forth there, there was some point and purpose to it. A man could learn how to handle them.'

And then he would talk endlessly about the stories of ships he had heard over the years, going back into the past to talk about the likes of the steam packet *Pulaski*, which went down off the coast of North Carolina with 128 people lost. Or men like Blackbeard, an English pirate whose boat the *Adventure* had tried to haul his flagship, *Queen Anne's Revenge*, off a sandbar where it had been stranded.

'A real rogue, him,' Nathan would say, spitting occasionally into the fireplace as he sucked his pipe. Occasionally a dark stain from this activity could be seen on his crumpled clothes. They were rarely ever ironed, fitting him as loosely as his skin. 'Even looking at him was chilling. He had this huge black beard which came right up to his eyes. He would tie this up in pigtails, even fasten small candles to their ends.'

Finlay laughed when he spoke about this. 'There was a man from our village who was a lot like that. The only difference is that it wasn't candles that brought a gleam to his beard. Only little bits of herring that got stuck there after he had finished eating.'

They giggled when he said this. Even Nathan's wife, Katja, laughed at the story, something she did very rarely. This might because she had been brought up speaking both German and Danish and was not that comfortable with English as a language. 'We were like that for the first years in coming here,' Mairead had sympathised with her once. 'But then we had some advantages over you. English was hammered into us at school.'

Katja nodded her head. 'The same happened in Southern Schleswig where I grew up. Many Danish speakers were there. They were all forced to learn German, whether they liked it or not.'

'The same might be happening again today,' Nathan said, 'now that Hitler's invaded Denmark.'

'Yes. There's a chance of that.' Katja frowned.

'Sorry. I shouldn't have mentioned that,' Nathan said. 'We're not supposed to talk about what's going on in Europe at the moment. Causes too much hurt.'

'I don't blame you for that.' Finlay nodded. 'I try not to think about it myself.'

'Okey-dokey,' Nathan declared, an expression that young Roddy had noted was often on their neighbour's lips. 'Let's move on.'

It was the tales of boats that most fascinated Roddy, not the war. His father would talk about the Mosquito Fleet, the huge number of skiffs, dinghies and motor launches that had thronged the mile-wide gap between the city and Windsor when he first arrived in Detroit all those years before.

'They were so crammed with beer and whisky that their gunwales were washed by water even on the calmest of days. Either that or they were loaded down with barrels filled with cash.'

He also spoke sometimes about how he, too, had gone fishing in boats from Port of Ness and Skigersta when he was young. It was the one time he and his brothers were at peace together, throwing out fishing lines from the small boats they occupied, standing near the sterns of the vessels with rods in their hand. They had even gone out to the isle of North Rona once, stepping around its shores, examining the foundations of houses where people from their native parish had once lived.

'A couple of German U-boats anchored there during the Great War, going out to catch some of the sheep that men in Ness left grazing in those parts,' he told Nathan and Roddy.

'They might be going there again now,' Nathan muttered, repeating a similar remark to the one he had made earlier.

'Yes, yes, that's true enough,' Finlay said, nodding. 'But best not to think about that. One reason why no one from home will be going there at the moment.'

Roddy's blue eyes sparkled when he heard these stories, conscious he had never even seen the sea his parents often talked about, mentioning its storms, rocks and beaches, the sheer size of the stretch of water that divided the continent where they now lived from the island on which they had been raised. In order to make up for this gap in his existence, he would often urge his father to take him to the centre of Detroit, to walk by the harbour near the Detroit Bridge, not far from the underwater tunnel and the Ambassador Bridge that now connected the city with both Canada and the town of Windsor a short stretch of water away. His fair hair waving in the breeze, Roddy would clutch his father's binoculars in his hands, looking out for the types of vessels Nathan mentioned in his talks, sometimes no longer seen on the water but stirred into existence once more in his words.

'Amazing how many I've caught sight of in my life,' the old man would declare, counting them out endlessly on his fat fingers. 'Paddle wheel steamboats. Tugboats. Launches. Skiffs. Ferries. Barges. Ocean liners. Battleships. Submarines. Cargo ships. I've even seen the ruins of things. The remains of bulkheads and wharves. A few shipwrecks.'

And then Roddy's mind would run through the list Nathan had mentioned, the ships that had been lost in the Great Lakes. He would recall names like the *Bannockburn*, the vessel named after a famous battle that took place between the Scots and English many centuries before. Though it had disappeared just after the turn of the century, it was said to still haunt the Great Lakes today. During times when snow and ice clamped its waters, its hull could be glimpsed, still carrying the cargo of 85,000 bushels of wheat it had borne when it disappeared, forty years before. Standing beside his father, Roddy would imagine he had spotted its shadow darkening the waters, creasing the waves as it journeyed onwards, defying time and its own destruction in its endless voyage.

Or it might be the *City of Bangor* he imagined seeing, the one in which his brother Hugh had taken an interest. Nathan had told them about the cargo of 202 Chrysler cars that had been salvaged from the vessel after it sank.

'I wonder if any were left on board,' Hugh said. 'We could go and try to find them. See if they're fit to drive these days.'

Or, too, there was the tale of the *Eastland*, which had rolled over on its side when it was tied to the dock in Chicago, killing more than 800 of those on board near the end of July in 1915. Roddy noticed his father's face screwing up when this was mentioned, his body beginning to shiver.

'Let's not go there,' Dad said. 'Too many memories. I've seen things like that before in my life.'

It was his mother who explained what he was talking about that time, how Finlay's father had been in Stornoway on the day in 1904 when some of the survivors of the *Norge* ship had been brought to the town, more than 600 having drowned after the vessel had hit a rock near Rockall. And later, on the very first day of 1919, his uncle had been among the over 200 men drowned on the *Iolaire* when the ship had struck the Beasts of Holm while returning home from the war.

'Both these days cast their shadows on your father's family,' his mother had said. 'A darkness they've never quite got over.'

There were other ships and stories, too, his father spoke about. There were times he would mention how he and Mairead had set sail on the *Metagama*, leaving their home island of Lewis all those years before. He mentioned the crowd that had crammed on the roof of the MacBrayne building, the psalm that had been sung, the bagpipes played, even the way he had overheard the Jews praying loudly on the deck after escaping the perils of their homeland.

'It was the first time I had ever been in the company of people who were very different from ourselves. Between blacks, Greeks, Southerners and the Irish, I've made up for a lot of that since.'

And then he laughed loudly to himself.

'And I'm not talking about your mother when I say that. Though I must admit I looked at her in a very different way from the way I usually did that day. Before then, I just thought of her as a wee girl in Cross school. One that came from South Dell. Something that made her very odd indeed.'

Mairead flapped a copy of the *Detroit News* in his direction when he said this, forgetting for a moment all the dark headlines about the war its pages carried.

'Oh, Finlay,' she laughed.

'It was being on the *Metagama* that made me change my attitude to her. I could see how kind she was. I never noticed that when I was back at home.'

'Was that when you fell in love with her?' Roddy asked, his blue eyes sparkling.

'It might have been,' Finlay chuckled, astonished at the question his son had asked. 'It might have been.'

Twenty-two

Finlay's forehead wrinkled a little when he said that about Mairead. It reminded him of what had drawn him to her on board the *Metagama*. He had noticed particularly how kind she was to George, the man who had lost his life while on board. It was something he hadn't been aware of when they had been together in school. He had been barely conscious of her personality back then, just the way she looked.

He hadn't noticed either the weight some people carried on the voyage till that happened, though he had seen it time and time again since, how some had found it difficult to adapt to their new lives in the city after they had crossed the Atlantic. There were certainly moments when he had felt like that, when it struck him how much the rhythm and pattern of each day in the garage felt much more monotonous than life on the croft.

Yet even though he often got fed up of his existence in Detroit, obtaining relief and release from a glass or two of whisky, gin or bourbon, he hadn't suffered as much as many who had left the islands around the same time as him. There was a man from some village on the west side of Lewis who had jumped off the Ambassador Bridge shortly after it had been built. There was a woman from South Uist who had leapt from the waterfront in the darkness, near where both the Underground Railroad and the Mosquito Fleet had crossed, never to be seen again. He shook his head, recalling how much talk there had been about her, how she had been employed as a housemaid by a gangster family in the prohibition era and had seen far too much of what was going on. 'Not sure if she actually fell or was pushed,' someone told him. 'Best not to ask.'

He bit his lip, preferring not to think about such matters. It was easier to consider those who had made successes of their years on this side of the Atlantic. Or even those who had returned home again, unable to withstand the differences of existing in, say, Manitoba or Michigan, compared to their old lives back on the island. At least they were safe and survived the ordeal.

And then Mairead jostled his shoulder, as if she was trying to break him out of the depths of his thoughts. 'Come on. Tell the boys a few stories about the boats you knew.'

'All right.'

Even then he stifled and censored what he had to say. There were so many boats from his own native district that had been lost over the years. He had heard the stories while working with his relatives in the blacksmith's. *Eathar Iain Chuidhsiadair* and the drowning of six men. *Eathar Aonghais Chaluim Ruaidh* and the loss of fishermen from Mairead's home village. The *Christina*, which had apparently been rammed by a boat from Buckie on the east coast of Scotland. The five Ness boats that had been lost in December 1862, a tale he remembered hearing from his uncle's lips: 'One of the greatest tragedies that ever affected this place, at least until the *Iolaire* came along.'

But Finlay never mentioned any of these. Instead, he talked about how a boat occupied by men from the village of Galson had disappeared, their vessel found upturned on the shoreline, a bonnet worn by one of the men lying near its stern.

'A wee while later, the rumours started that there were several men from Lewis stranded somewhere in the West Indies, that an island sailor had heard them speak while he walked through a port in Barbados. That, some time after that, one of the missing men had come home to his house in Galson. He stood outside its walls in the darkness, only to hear his wife's voice talking to another man inside. He turned away then, going back to Stornoway and later the mainland of Scotland. "Too late to do anything about it," he apparently told someone he met there. "I couldn't tear up her life by walking towards her. I had to step away.'"

He spoke, too, about a story he had heard from a Harrisman about how a boat skippered by Alan Morrison, a Lewis sailor, had sunk on its way to the isle of Scalpay, where his fiancée, Annie Campbell, lived. His body had been washed up on the shoreline of the largest of the Shiant Islands, off the east coast of Harris.

'She went mad with grief after that. A while later, they took her dead body out of Scalpay on a boat, planning to bury her in the south of Harris, in the sandy soil there. When they did this, a storm blew up. The boat was in danger of sinking, so much so that they decided they had no choice but to throw the coffin overboard. A few weeks later, they found it again. She had landed in the exact same spot where Alan had been found. It was as if the two of them were designed to be together for all eternity.'

He looked up at Mairead, seeing her eyes glaze over with tears. There was a glint, too, in the visions of both their sons.

'Sorry,' he muttered.

In order to try and cheer them up, he began to sing the words of a song that had been on his lips during the first days he had been on board the *Metagama*, when those around him had hammered out its loud, insistent rhythms on the table in front of them, tapping its notes.

'Ic iarla nam bratach bàna
'Ic iarla nam bratach bàna
'Ic iarla nam bratach bàna
Chunna' mi do long air sàile

Hi 'illean beag ho ill o ro
Hi 'illean beag ho ill o ro
Hi 'illean beag ho ill o ro
Hu hoireann o hu o eileadh.

The son of the earl of the white banners
The son of the earl of the white banners
The son of the earl of the white banners
I saw your longship on the sea.

As he did this, he watched Mairead and his children clap their hands in the rhythm of his voice, glad to see them cheerful once again.

Twenty-three

It was cars that drew Hugh's attention. Mairead was aware of this because, each time they walked down a street together, he would notice every vehicle that passed by, pointing them out with his finger. He had the same sparkle in his blue eyes as his older brother Roddy possessed, though his hair was darker, his shoulders a little broader.

'A Ford Model A,' he would say.

'A LaSalle Coupe.'

'Cord 812 Convertible.'

'Chrysler Model 70.'

Sometimes he might even recite the numberplates on these cars, imitating the sounds he had sometimes heard when his father sang a verse or two of *Puirt à beul* in his home.

And then there were the days he'd spot a strange car in the distance. 'I want to go and see what it's like,' he demanded.

'We haven't got time to go there.'

'But I want to! I want to!' he yelled, stamping his feet again and again on the sidewalk. 'I need to see it!'

She tugged his hand to draw him away. 'No. No. You can't! We haven't got time.'

'Please! Please! Please!'

She knew where he had obtained both these skills and temperament. Not her family line but Finlay's, passed on through the generations from men like his cousins, working in the blacksmith's store in her own village of South Dell. She had been there a few times with her father when she was young, looking at the forge and anvil, the range of tools that were on display, her neighbours Tormod, Murdo and Calum working away – the last man crippled by some illness he had caught while in Liverpool on his way to war. She recalled feeling a little choked by the smoke of the coal fire, the blackness of the soot that could be seen in so many corners of the room. It was a reaction that remained with her. There were times when she put her scarf to her lips in order to avoid gulping down the smoke of a passing lorry with a broken exhaust. She also had seen Finlay raging, slamming doors and cursing as he went along, both inside and outside their home. It was something that happened far too often, his rage increasing with the years.

Hugh's interests were the same as his father's. Sometimes she would find the boy on his haunches or knees, stretched out on the pavement, looking at the underside of some vehicle or other he had noticed parked nearby. He was fascinated by the variety of their size and shapes. Trucks. Vans. Cars. Buses. The many different vehicles that helped to fashion the roads and buildings of Detroit. He looked at them all, taking in the curve of every wheel, the intricacy of each engine, as if he were trying to take a photograph of each detail. There were questions, too, he directed towards his father, especially about the work he was doing since the beginning of the war in Europe, now that Detroit was part of the US Arsenal of Democracy, as FDR called it again and again.

'What's it like working on a jeep?' he would ask Finlay. 'A tank? A lorry?'

Finlay did his best to answer, talking about the weight of each part of these vehicles as they were lowered down towards him, the different sensations he experienced when he saw a tank commander's hatch, turret, side armour or tracks in front of him; how all the time he would think of its purpose, being sent to Europe to help Britain fight against Germany.

'I sometimes think of my home village of Swainbost when I'm working on it, how one of the lads from there might be sitting in it someday, heading for the fighting. The thought makes my skin creep.' He shrugged, shaking his head. 'And then I feel a little guilty, thinking of the way that life is getting better for us in this city. Ever since the war started. I feel like I'm profiting from the misery of my own people.'

'At least we can depend on your money now,' Mairead said, thinking of all the years when their income was low. It was even this that had made them decide not to have more than two children – both sons, for all that she had often longed for a daughter. 'We need to be sure we can feed another mouth,' Finlay said. 'It's not as if we're living on a croft where we can grow food or allow a sheep or cow to graze. That's not an option here.'

Mairead sighed. It was one of the few reasons that nowadays she regretted ever leaving Lewis. The sight of green stalks of potatoes. Peat for the fireplace. Sheep on a stretch of grass. But despite these occasional feelings, she recognised that over the last few years she had seen her life improving again and again. A new and comfortable bed in their bedroom. Armchairs where they could feel comfortable. A car outside their door. A jingle in her purse. Both her and Finlay obtaining thicker wage packets than before. Sums that enabled her to open a special bank account for her brother Murdo, which he could get access to when the war came to an end. It made it easier to behave like Lot and his daughters, succeeding in looking ahead of her rather than glancing back at the existence they had left behind.

'It's good that it's all changed now. Even if it did need a war for that to happen,' she said to Finlay.

But she knew there was one thing that he disliked about the changes that the war had brought: there were far more people crowding the streets of Detroit than there had been even a few years before. Blacks from the Southern states, using the demand for workers as an opportunity to flee their homes and the hard, poorly paid work they had been compelled to do there. Greeks. Italians. Irish. Even some of his fellow Scots travelling south from Canada to find better-paid jobs in the city. They ducked and swerved as they strolled down the sidewalk, giving people little space or room.

'My pockets might be jingling, but my nerves are too,' he said once after a stroll round the centre of the city. 'I feel I'm being jostled every step of the way.'

'Just keep your head and eyes down,' Mairead said. 'Don't look at anyone in the face.'

'Oh, I know that. But sometimes even doing that won't save you.'

'It might. I've had loads of practice over the years.' Mairead frowned. 'Even way back in Toronto. Men talking behind your back, saying things about the shape of your body, the way you walk and move. Even when they're speaking in foreign languages, you know what they're talking about. Their eyes, their tone of voice, even the way they spit out their words sometimes. You suffer it in silence wherever you go.' And then she shivered. 'God knows I've even heard the likes of you and Nathan doing that sort of thing.'

She was talking about their neighbour, with whom Finlay was spending more and more of his time. In some ways, Nathan was a very pleasant and kind individual. He would sometimes provide them with coffee, give their sons cake or chocolate, an ice cream or two; yet some of the things he said could make Mairead uncomfortable, reminding her of shadows both in this city and country with which she was largely unfamiliar at home.

'Not very often,' Finlay said, in his own defence.

'Aye. Sometimes it's only when black women are around.' She paused for a moment before speaking again. 'We treat these people even worse than the tinkers when they used to come to Druim Fraoch on the edge of the village. Remember that? We used to take rusty padlocks out of our home and lock our doors for the first time in years. Some people stood guard over their peat stacks, in case they came along. And then we wondered why they were nasty and unpleasant to us. As if they had any other option. As if we hadn't sown the seeds ourselves for their behaviour. We've got no one to blame for the worst of their antics but ourselves.'

'Mairead …'

'What?' Mairead looked in his direction, watching the way he shook his head at her comments.

There was no doubt that she had changed a lot over the last few months, especially now that she had started working in a discount drugstore, where she was employed a few days a week. She had listened to the women who were customers there, noting how, unlike some of the females she had lived alongside on the island, they were unable to stay quiet when their husbands said something with which they disagreed. It had begun to alter her. She no longer bit her lip when she disagreed with him.

'I'm going to the restroom,' he muttered. 'I hope you'll be back to normal by the time I come back.'

'Perhaps … perhaps. But I think we should be careful of being too much in the company of the likes of Nathan. He's a

good man in some ways but he is in danger of poisoning people's minds.'

'I'll do my best. But' – he shrugged his shoulders – 'there's
few enough people around here that we can speak to. We can't
ignore Nathan. He lives next door. He helps to look after our
house whenever we need it. There's no escaping him and Katja.'

'We can but try ... We don't want our sons to start imitating
his views on certain things. It might be dangerous for them.'

Finlay shrugged again as he headed to the restroom. 'They
like him.'

'Whether they do or not.'

Yet it was not just the proximity of her neighbour that
made Mairead nervous. There was much else. She shook each
time she saw people calling out in the city streets to people
who looked different. She had even heard suffered it herself
one or twice, when a Glaswegian who had moved to Detroit
had called her a 'teuchter' and 'yokel' and began to imitate the
sound of the bagpipes when he heard her voice.

'*Skirl-skirl-whee-whoo-skirl ...*'

Or else some had seen her as a 'Jock' who either grasped
onto each coin with tight fingers, never letting it go, or were in
charge of the trade unions to be found in Detroit's car factories.

'Gi'es some cash,' they might say, reciting a few lines of verse.
'There's Scots and rats the whole world o'er and, Lord, they've
had their fill. One taks the crumbs from aff the floor. The other
raks the till.'

She bridled at all of this. Especially the behaviour of the
Detroit police. Like the blacks, many of them had come from
the Southern states, places like Georgia, Louisiana, Alabama.
They had brought many of the attitudes of their former homes
with them on that journey. They swaggered up to the black

people they encountered in alleys and streets, a cigarette perched between their lips, a baton underneath their arm.

'What the hell are you doing here?' they asked even the most respectable-looking men and women. 'Looking for something to swipe or pinch?'

And if their fingers clenched or lips curled in response, the officer shoved their shoulders or push them around. Sometimes a knuckler adorned the policeman's fists when he did this, protection against the possibility their victims might retaliate.

'Who do you think you are? Bloody Joe Louis?' he said, referring to the black boxer who was, perhaps, the city's most famous citizen, having become the World Heavyweight Champion just before the war. 'Be careful. Or we might send you back to where he came from years ago. Where was that?'

'Georgia. Mississippi. Tennessee.'

'Time to go back there if you can't bloody behave. It would keep these streets a lot safer if you did.'

In response, these black people bowed their heads, muttering an apology for the way they had reacted to the approach of the policeman.

'Sorry, sir. Sorry, officer.'

They walked away with their heads down, restraining the anger they clearly felt, shuffling along Michigan Avenue or whichever street it was. Mairead used to watch as they did this, feeling sorry for them and all they had suffered. She recalled once meeting a young white woman who had noted her troubled expression when an incident like this occurred in the discount drugstore where she worked. A black man had been refused service when he came to the counter. Her boss, Barrington, had been responsible for that, his thin lips barely concealing the row of big teeth in his mouth, his bald head bowed as his voice hissed in the customer's direction.

'We don't serve you people drugs like that in here.'

'Why not?'

'It's a way of keeping us all safe.'

Mairead shook her head, not knowing what drug he was talking about. It wasn't the first time she had seen him act in this way, refusing black customers goods without providing any real explanation for his behaviour. 'We have got to make sure that decent, respectable people feel comfortable when they come in here,' he declared once. 'And that sometimes means closing our counter to certain folk.'

Mairead said nothing until the young woman approached her, clearly annoyed at what she had seen.

'It's terrible the way these people are treated,' the woman frowned. 'It's as if they're still slaves.'

'I know,' Mairead muttered.

'There'll be an explosion someday if it keeps up.'

She shivered, fearing the words might be true; conscious, too, how they echoed those she had heard once or twice on her neighbour Nathan's lips, even if his viewpoint was very different, prophesying that the day would come when the blacks would be expelled from the city. 'Send them back to the farmlands or even farther. They're not fit for a life in the factories here.' But she said nothing, neither to Nathan nor the young woman. Instead, she walked away from the woman in the store, noting in her own head how unconventional she looked. Her hair was short, skirt also above her knees; all in all, a way of dressing that would have been utterly unacceptable in her childhood home, where a woman's hair was clasped tight below a headscarf, her skirt raised only a few inches above her ankles. She was clearly one of those whom Nathan described in his usual distasteful way. She had heard their son Hugh repeat insulting words recently, and she had reacted in a way that was unusual for her, slapping his backside.

'Don't say those words. Don't say these words.'

'Why not?' he yelled, slamming his feet again and again on the floor. 'I've heard Dad use them.'

'You sure?' She faltered when he said this, uncertain whether or not her son was telling the truth.

'Yes. A few times when he's driving. When one of them steps out from the sidewalk. Some other days too.'

'It doesn't mean you can do it.'

'Why not? If Dad does it—'

'Because I don't like it. I'm not allowing you to do it in front of me.'

'I don't see why not. A lot of the kids at school use it too,' he yelled. 'Why am I not allowed to do so?'

'That doesn't make it right.'

She shivered as she thought about this later. She knew that she had heard a number of insults about black people slipping from Finlay's lips, especially when he'd taken a drink and was in Nathan's company. They would echo each other's talk, nodding their heads throughout most conversations, especially when they turned to the subject of Nathan's former neighbours in the South.

'We chased them all out of Wilmington at the end of the nineteenth century! Best thing we ever did. We'll probably have to do the same here one day.'

'Who knows?' Finlay said. 'Who knows?'

'The day will come. The day will come.' Nathan sucked on his cigarette, its smoke whirling like a cloud around the wave on his head as he indulged in repeating a prophecy that had passed his lips a few times. 'There's too many of them crammed into places like black Bottom and Paradise Valley. All these streets east of Woodward Avenue filled with rats and garbage. Sooner or later, the explosion will take place.'

Finlay frowned. 'I hope you're wrong about that.'

'But you fear I might be right.' Nathan's eyes glinted.

'Perhaps …' Finlay shrugged his shoulders.

'You know I'm right!' he cheered, pouring out another glass of bootleg from one of the many bottles he had stored within his home since the days of prohibition.

'Perhaps …' Finlay said again. 'Perhaps.'

The only time she could recall them disagreeing was the night they listened together to Joe Louis and Max Schmeling's fight on the wireless, the second one that took place in New York. When Joe Louis floored the German within two minutes, Finlay cheered, his feet dancing as he stood up from the fireside chair.

'Great! He's got the Hun! Wonderful stuff!'

Nathan looked in his direction. 'That's because you're still carrying the last war on your shoulders.'

'Back where I come from, it would be a hard thing to shake off.'

'I can see why. But you have to do it.'

'With what's in the news at the moment, I doubt it. I've seen too many of my own people killed by the Germans in the last war to think like that.'

Nathan stayed quiet, looking at him before he finally shrugged. 'Let's agree to disagree about that one.'

Finlay nodded. 'Yes. Let's.'

But despite their differences, her husband's attitudes to black people were still all too clear. She noticed it in the way

Finlay sometimes spoke about them, especially in the company of Nathan. He called them 'dingy doo', a phrase based on the Gaelic expression *daoine dubh*, muttering the expression occasionally when he saw them while driving, especially when he was exasperated with one or more of them racing across the street.

'*Amadais*,' he would say. '*Daoine gorach*.'

She would sigh in disapproval when he spoke like that, wondering if the mood he displayed at moments like this was an unexpected legacy of the existence he had led at home. He had often complained about it when he was younger; how surly and bad-tempered his family had been to one another; how his father had gone into petty rages about the most trivial matters. There were times he blamed it on the old man's experience in the Great War, how his mind and mood had been affected when he was on two ships that had been sunk. Yet Finlay was all too often showing these same characteristics. He would complain about the neighbours or lose his temper with either her or their sons from time to time. His movement around the house would be punctuated by the slamming of doors, the pounding of a table.

'A man needs peace when he gets home from work,' he would declare. 'And I never bloody get it!'

His temper was worse on the days when he had to deal with certain people, like blacks, Mexicans, Irish, Germans, the list varying from day to day. Especially when he read the news about what was going on in the war in Europe. He would snarl and throw the paper away, asking the same question again and again.

'How long are the Yanks going to stand in silence about this?'

He received his answer to that question a few days later. An hour or two after Mairead had received a telegram from her brother that her father had passed away, Finlay discovered from those around him that the Japanese had just bombed Pearl Harbour.

'We'll be told we'll be at war any day now,' he said, crumpling the newspaper someone had handed him. 'Let's hope we don't have to go through what people like my dad suffered. Let's hope I'm too old to be called up.'

'Or too valuable,' Mairead said. 'They're going to need more engineers around these parts if the war continues.'

It took a moment or two for Finlay to respond to her words, but finally he nodded, as if he was prepared to admit that, for once, she was probably right.

Twenty-four

Murdo had tried to call his father a few times that morning, his voice echoing through the house as it had done on a few occasions recently. The old man often started the night by having difficulty sleeping and began the morning by doing the opposite.

'Are you awake? Are you awake?'

It was only after Murdo had shouted ten times or more that he finally stepped into the room, finding the old man's body coiled within blankets. Even from a glance, it was clear he had passed away a few hours before, his wrinkled face so passive and still. On a December morning like this, he often shivered and shook with the cold until he came down to sit in his usual chair by the stove.

There was a lot to be done. The first thing he knew he had to do was send a telegram to his sister. It meant a visit to the post office, aware that this was the only way he could get news to her at the moment. When he was there, he heard someone talk about the Japanese and Pearl Harbour, but he barely listened. All that talk of war seemed scarcely important compared to what had happened within his own home. He knew the grief that would overwhelm Mairead, no matter what words he chose. He could picture her trembling and shaking, the piece of paper tight within her hands. As a result, he kept the message tight and close, not letting his emotions slip too deep into what he had to say.

Sorry to tell you Father passed away last night. Love, Murdo.

When he finished doing this, he felt himself tremble, not only because of his grief and loss but also at the prospect of being alone in the house without his father. It was something he had feared for a long time, but now that it had happened, the road ahead seemed more desolate and emptier than he had ever imagined it being before. It led not to any particular destination but circled bogs and moorland, wetter and more difficult to journey across at this time of year than any other.

His neighbours helped him out. Tormod, the blacksmith who lived a few doors away, came with him to visit the minister in the nearby village of Cross, and also to see the man a few miles away in Eoropie who built coffins for the bodies of the people of the parish who had passed away. Tormod was also by Murdo's side when Mairead's telegram arrived, fingers clasping his shoulder when he opened the envelope to discover the message within.

> *Sorry to hear this news. Thinking of you and praying for you.*
> *Love, Mairead, Roddy, Hugh and Finlay.*

The women of the village helped too. They came to his home with scones and oatcakes that they made for him in these days of loss of sorrow. Among them was Dolina, who brought a rabbit stew to his door, leaving it in his outstretched fingers as he stood there. He looked at her, recalling how she had done this so often when his mother had passed away, bringing him a gift of food day after day.

'You all right?' he asked.

She didn't answer for a long time, even when he gazed directly into her face. For the first time, he noticed there was a bruise upon her cheek, tears filling her eyes.

'I'm fine, fine, fine,' she answered. 'Fine, fine, fine.'

She turned away from him, clasping her dark scarf tightly against her skin, as if she was guarding her bruise once again, making sure no one else in the village even glimpsed its existence.

Twenty-five

'Why did you never call either of your boys Donald?'

'Sorry?'

'Why did you never call either of your boys Donald?' Ina repeated the question she had asked once before, the morning after she arrived from her home in Guelph, Ontario. 'It was the name of both their grandads.'

'We thought about it.' Mairead grinned.

'And why didn't you do it?' Ina asked once more.

Mairead shrugged, still smiling. 'Well, I decided it wasn't a good idea. We came here to make a fresh start in our lives, not to endlessly look back at the past. Giving our son a name that had nothing to do with where we came from seemed a good idea for that reason.'

Ina's bottom lip jutted outwards in thought. 'Most people want to keep connections with the islands.'

'Not everyone. I always remember what that man from Bragar said when we left Lewis. "What did I owe that island? Nothing but poverty and hurt." There were a few who were delighted to escape it.'

'And quite a few, too, who've decided to return there. There's always a mix.'

'We held on … Besides, we're very lucky not to have called either of our sons Donald.'

'Why?'

'Nowadays there's a cartoon duck been given the name. Neither of our sons would have escaped that. They tell me that there's this boy whose parents called him Donald. His dad came from the Highlands. Guess what the other lads shout after him?'

'Quack, quack, quack?'

'Where'syourcapandbowtie, Tonald?'

The two women laughed, relaxed once more in each other's company.

'Aye. I never thought of that,' Ina said, grinning. 'You must be very glad to have never christened him that name. The poor souls that have it. I know quite a few of them.'

'Who knows how they suffer?'

And then Ina did what she so often did in conversation on the various occasions she had come to visit them: recount stories of what had happened to several of the people that had journeyed alongside them on the *Metagama*.

Ina worked in the office of a brewery in Ontario. It was something that she occasionally whispered about, saying that she had sometimes been in contact with a man called Rocco Perri, especially during the prohibition years in the States. 'They called him "King of the Bootleggers". Canada's own version of Al Capone.' And then she would bite her lip tightly, anxious that not another word on the subject should slip out, and she'd return once more to her favourite topic, the ones she had spoken and written about almost since her arrival on these shores.

'You know there was a fellow from Uig who used to spend hours and hours trying to blow out the light in his lodgings. It took over a week before this man from Point pointed out there was a switch.' She chuckled a little before adding more to the tale. 'Goodness knows how long he took to be able to flush the toilet.'

'And then there's Angie Morrison, from Back. You know he's got a job working on the Woodbine Racecourse near Toronto. Really happy for the man. Remember how he told us that he was worried that he wouldn't be able to work with horses anymore in Canada?'

'Yes, I remember him saying that.'

'Well, his dreams have come true. Though the racehorses he works with now are very different from those on the croft.'

She bowed her head for a moment, her white hair almost the same shade as the snow they had seen the previous few winters in Detroit, before she spoke again.

'There's a woman called Joan, from Bayble in Point, who sneaked across the border from Toronto to go to Georgia or South Carolina to work in the cotton and corn there. Apparently, she missed working in the fields like she did as a child and decided to go there. She was given quite a welcome. Especially as so many black people down there are moving north to work in the factories.' She laughed quietly to herself. 'Trust someone from that part of the island to go in the opposite direction from everyone else. They always were an awkward bunch.'

She paused for an instant before beginning her account once more.

'And then there's Alasdair Macleod, from Achmore. I've told you about him before. He got married to a woman in Manitoba and has now gone back home to the village with her. Someone told me that his bride belonged to a tribe called the Cree. That will start a lot of gossip back on the island.'

'You think she'll find it easy to settle down there?'

'Who knows? She won't exactly be alone there. There's one or two of her kind gone back to the crofts with our menfolk. And a few men who left their country wives in Alberta or Manitoba before going back to the islands and finding the real thing there.'

'Oh, I didn't know that.'

'And then she would list the names of a few others who had chosen Cree women, or those from some other tribe, and either moved to Lewis or one of the other islands. Before she completed this task, Mairead interrupted her.

'It must be difficult for all of them,' she said.

'What do you mean?'

'Well, it was hard enough for the likes of us to move to a country like this, where there's a huge mix of people with different tongues and backgrounds. It must be even harder for them, to move to a place where just about everyone looks and thinks the same.'

And then Ina continued to speak about other matters, the one or two islanders whose difficulty in adjusting to a new existence had made them either take to drink or put an end to their lives; those, too, who had profited from their voyages across the Atlantic.

'There's a fellow from South Uist who has become a Superintendent of Police in Chicago ... Another soul from Carloway who's become a top banker in Montreal ...'

***

A short time after that conversation, Mairead began once again to read a letter her brother had written before both the war and the death of her father. It was one she looked at from time to time, a way of keeping in touch with Murdo after letters from him became less and less regular, especially after their dad became ill and he had to spend some time nursing the old man, a situation where he had to spend more time on croft-work, cooking and preparing food.

I'm not the best at that, he had declared. *Every time I boil fish, it's got no flavour left when I put it on the plate.*

This letter, however, had been different from most he had written over the years. Instead of just telling her the latest news about their neighbours and relatives, he had instead written a long epistle about how much both their village and district had changed over the decades, and he talked about those islanders who had returned home from places like the States and Canada.

They bore everyone with their stories. They go on for hours about all they've seen on the other side of the Atlantic. They talk about icebergs they've seen, wolves or polar bears they noticed while they were over there. One minute they're yarning away about some factory they worked in. The next, they're lecturing us about some snowstorm they've been in, how the icicles that hung from the gutters of buildings looked like the blades of giant scythes, able to cut through people if they ever fell. They talk too about how the unmelted snow on sidewalks resembled mountains they were forced to climb. Or it might be the amount of water that floods down the Niagara Falls, or a fight in the streets they stumbled across, or the illegal rum and whisky that's gushed down their throats, making them sick for days afterwards.

And then there's all the quarrels they're having with their brothers and sisters about who owns a stretch of croftland or shoreline. Everyone's temper has increased since they came home. You can hear the shouting as you go past certain houses. 'We never expected you to come home!' they yell. 'We didn't think we'd ever see you back here!' Once I even heard the question 'why the hell didn't you stay where you were? You were making loads more dollars there than you'll ever have the chance of making here!'

There are others, too, who cannot stop complaining about feeling cramped at home. They keep moaning about how

*there's only one town and it's miles away, that all the houses
in the villages around them all look the same. They're bored
and restless most of the time and keep whingeing on and on
about it. Some of them don't talk about anything else.*

So, if you ever decide to come home, don't see it as the same
place it was before. It isn't in so many ways. The Great War and
the *Iolaire* changed it a lot. So have people leaving it to go to
places like Canada and America and then coming home.

Mairead would sometimes smile or laugh when she read
that letter. It made her glad that she had not behaved like Lot's
wife since she left the island, looking back again and again at
where she had come from. For all the troubles that sometimes
obscured her view, it was far better to look forwards.

Twenty-six

'You know there were a couple of ships crammed with Americans that went down near your dad's part of the world?' Nathan told Finlay one day.

'No.'

'Off a place called Islay,' Nathan continued, his pronunciation of that last word making Finlay smile. He transformed the 's' into a 'z', mispronounced the rest too. 'Two boats. One called the *Tuscania* where over 200 troops died. Another called the *Otranto* where around 600 drowned. Some of them came from Wilmington, just like me. Others came from other parts of Appalachia and far beyond. Kicked a real hole into the life of our part of the world. Put some of the folk there right off the whole bloody notion of the war. Not the first time we felt we were crazy getting involved in it.'

He took another swig of coffee he had been given, letting it swirl down his throat before speaking again.

'That's true, isn't it?' He looked over in Finlay's direction.

'Aye. It is.' In Detroit, he had met a few people from Islay, and virtually every other island off the coast of Scotland. Some had arrived there in a different way from the people of the Outer Hebrides. Instead of going to Canada, they had travelled to places like New York State. Apparently, there was a man called MacLean who had once been a gardener in Islay who now lived there in a big house. His wife had built a basement, where people from their native island stayed until they made up their minds where to go. 'It's a bit like a chain gang,' the Islay man who had spoken about this had joked. 'One that sprawls across the Atlantic and spreads to the Great Lakes.' The same man had spoken, too, about the sinking of the *Otranto* and how it had affected the people of his home community. 'The people of Islay spent days burying the corpses that were washed up near their homes. It had one hell of an effect on them.'

'It had a hell of an effect on the people of Georgia too,' Nathan said, nodding. 'Lots of them were on board that ship. Lots of people lost husbands, sons, fathers.'

'You aren't unique in that,' Finlay said, thinking back to his own childhood. It was probably his years at sea that had caused some of his father's failings, the way he would rage at his sons. He had been on two ships that went down, and one was in the Dardanelles. The HMS *Goliath* proved less strong and powerful than its name suggested when three torpedoes from a Turkish vessel powered their way towards it. Over 570 men who were on board had perished. He had been one of the 180 or so who had survived, but there were times when he had been somehow still immersed in the darkness of that time. Sometimes he would fall asleep by the fireside and wake up sweating, rambling about some boy he had seen drowning.

'Torquil Macleod from Invergordon or thereabouts. He was only fourteen or so. I saw him sinking into the water and stretched out my hand to save him, but he went down, impossible for me to reach. They caught him on another boat, but it was much too late.' He would shake his head, as if trying to chase him from his thoughts. 'I remember thinking – just for a second – that he was one of my own sons. And I had just let him down badly, allowed him to slip away.'

And then he would stamp his heels, as if attempting to crush the memory of that moment, squashing it below his sole. 'Are you still sitting there watching me, boy? Don't you think you should go out and do some work?'

It was this that had made life with his father difficult. There was a constant unpredictability about the man. Neither Finlay nor his brothers could ever tell how he might react from moment to moment to what was happening around him. One minute, there might be laughter. The next, there could be rage.

But it was different from that with the likes of Nathan. Finlay could relax with him after a day's work. They might even sip a few whiskies together, each of them doing this out of sight of their wives, who sometimes met in the kitchen. Nathan was a good reason for staying in these parts, but it wasn't the only one. There were good schools in the area. Julia Ward Howe Elementary School, to which both boys had gone when young. Foch Middle School and Southeastern High, to which they travelled now that they were older.

There were also places like Boblo Island not far away, to which the family sometimes travelled for entertainment, going there on boats like the *Columbia* or *Ste Claire*. At the annual gathering organised by the St Andrew's Society of Detroit, they would gather there with hundreds of others, including quite a few who had sailed on the *Metagama*, *Marloch* or *Canada*. Gaelic songs familiar to them since childhood would echo round the island, their fingers tapping out the rhythms of *Bratach Bana* as they had done when they sailed on the *Metagama*. Or they'd singing new and less familiar songs, like *Balaich an Iasgaich* or *Faili Faili Faili Oro*, written by fellow islesmen in exile in places like Duluth or Manitoba before they travelled homewards again. Both Mairead and Finlay mouthed the words, becoming more familiar with them as each year of exile passed by.

Faili, faili, faili oro
Faili, faili, faili oro

Faili, faili, faili oro
'S cian nan cian bho dh'fhàg mi Leòdhas .
Faili, faili, faili oro
Faili, faili, faili oro
Faili, faili, faili oro
It's been so long since I left Lewis.

And then there were those that thronged around the Highland dancers or clapped their hands or stamped their feet when the pipe-band marched past, recalling their own home-places back in Scotland as they did so, singing songs that were familiar to them from their childhood years before.

Hark when the night is falling
Hear! hear the pipes are calling,
Loudly and proudly calling,
Down through the glen.
There where the hills are sleeping,
Now feel the blood a-leaping,
High as the spirits
Of the old Highland men ...

Throughout some of this fervour, Finlay watched Mairead slip away with the boys, taking them to the swan boats that were found on a pool on the island, gathering on the benches before the plumage where the captain was concealed. Or else, when they were young, they might head for the rollercoaster or dodgems, their heads reeling with excitement each time they stepped towards or away from a ride. Roddy was especially excited by all of this – the evidence for his interest even seen in the travel poster that was pinned to the wall of his bedroom, one that showed a man soaring over Acapulco Bay on a kite carried on the back of a speedboat.

'Flight and water ...' he said once. 'My favourite mix.'

Yet it was the two boats that took them to the island which most fascinated Roddy. Finlay would watch his son pace around their decks, examining each detail of the ships throughout the hour and more it took them to travel the twenty miles or so from Woodward Avenue, where the ship left the city to go the island.

On one occasion, he listened to the blast of the steam whistle and turned to his father and mother. 'Does this remind you of being on the *Metagama*?'

'Not much,' Finlay confessed. 'A lot less water both ahead and below.' He laughed for a moment before referring to another location where he'd been a few years before, a fellow Lewisman who worked there taking him down into its depths. 'The salt mine in the city reminded me in some ways a whole lot more. The whiff that was all around me there brought the shoreline of Swainbost back to mind.'

'And the surroundings here don't exactly look like Stornoway,' Mairead said, smiling. 'Still, stepping on a boat reminds me of how long it took getting here all these years ago. Days and nights on end.'

Finlay watched Mairead shiver as she said this, thinking – as she so often did – of the death of George that took place on the vessel; the icebergs they had passed as they approached the Canadian shoreline were like memorials for him in her memory.

'One day I'll make the voyage back for you,' Roddy grinned. 'Who knows? I might take the two of you along with me.'

'I doubt that,' Mairead said. 'Once in a lifetime is enough to make a crossing like that.'

'Mind you, quite a few decided to return,' Finlay added. 'Me and your mother were some of the exceptions.'

'I know.'

Looking at their son, Finlay had the feeling Roddy might be an exception too. Someday he was likely to sail across the Atlantic, voyaging across that vast stretch of water on some vessel or other, making his way in the direction of their former home. He felt excitement surge through him as he thought of his son making that journey, walking once again across the quayside that the *Metagama* had left many years before.

Twenty-seven

Roddy felt comfortable walking and watching boats. fFom a young age, he was obsessed by the ships he observed making their way on the Detroit River, taking notes of their names on the pad he crammed into his pocket. He showed these traits even when he was on the boats taking him to the islands near the city. On his way to Boblo Island, he would stand gazing from the main deck down into the engine room, noting the power and steely brightness of the shafts, how the crams slowly warmed up, turning round and round to ensure the ship was on its way. Once or twice, he even helped the sailors casting off the lines, allowed to do this by a man his father knew from Lewis who now worked on the ship. He listened to his stories, how that Hebridean had – like a few others – fished out of Stornoway for a few years.

'There are days when I miss that life,' the older man would reflect. 'Every day brought something new.'

He had the same fascination with Belle Island, also not far from the city. Sometimes the young lad walked across the bridge with his friends towards the island, visiting the aquarium that was there, seeing its fountains and the red-white-and-blue flag-shaped flower bed, its horse paths and beach. At other times he took the ferry or went to the island's lighthouse or waterways, getting money from hiring a canoe or kayak while he was there.

'It's like going to your home in Lewis,' he told his dad one day.

Oh, it's very different to that,' Finlay said, grinning. 'There's far more of a crowd gathering there on some summer days than ever stepped out at home. Far more likely to be a big fight too. All these blacks and Southerners.'

His father's words were at their most true one hot and sultry midsummer's day when Roddy contemplated visiting the island with some of his schoolfriends. Instead, he stood on the waterfront seeing smoke rising from the shores of the island, hearing the sound of gunfire, the roars and yells of crowds of men, echoing from the bridge where a mob was clearly gathering – both blacks and whites racing towards each other, throwing stones, timber and wooden barrels, anything that came to hand.

His mother's words came to him as he watched what was going on, the way that the waterfront around him was beginning to fill up with angry white men, many not much older than himself. 'If there's ever trouble, get right back to us,' she had said. 'Don't hang around.'

He wasn't the only boy who had been told to do that. David, one of his classmates, turned round to him and said only slightly different words to those he had heard before on his mother's lips. 'We'd better get the hell out of here. My dad will give us blazes if we don't.'

'Okay.'

Both he and a few of his schoolfriends took their parents' advice, racing from the waterfront and the city centre, heading towards the nearest streetcar going in the direction of their homes.

Some of the others continued to hang around.

Twenty-eight

It was Mairead's boss, Barrington, who noticed that something was happening in the centre of the city that day. One moment, he was standing outside the drugstore doorway, as he often did when he needed a smoke. A few moments later, he was back in the store once again, his face and voice blustering, the stub of his cigarette still crumpled in his hand.

'There's smoke rising from the centre of the city,' he mumbled. He stammered for a moment before speaking again. 'Loads of sirens too. Fire engines. Ambulances. Cop cars. Something's going on.'

Mairead shook, the impact of his words like a punch in her guts, one that released a cry of fear and anxiety. She tumbled towards the door, looking out into the distance to the city centre, where countless fires were burning. She could see plumes of smoke rising from buildings she barely recognised, the hot blaze, too, of flames. She had barely seen the like since that night she had been on the *Metagama*, telling herself not to look back but unable to avoid the sight of the bonfires on the coastline, identifying the places she had known in her life before the voyage.

'South Dell ... Swainbost ... Knockaird ...'

And then she could see Reverend MacQueen in her head, looking intensely at his congregation through the thickness of his eyebrows, his fists upon the pulpit, reading the verse from the Bible that had stayed with her over the years. 'As the smoke of the country went up as the smoke of a furnace, she looked back then behind Lot and she became a pillar of salt, punished for her indecision, for her longing to return to that city which had been destroyed by God.'

She swirled her gaze away, as if the plumes of smoke in the centre were some kind of repetition of what Lot had turned his back on when 'it rained fire and brimstone from Heaven and destroyed them all'. As she did so, she heard Barrington mutter behind her back.

'We're in the middle of a war, and the blacks in this city are acting like this.'

'It may not just be the blacks,' she heard one of the customers say. 'Some of our white kids are thugs too.'

'Hell, no … Hell, no,' Barrington repeated. 'It'll be the blacks who started this nonsense. No doubt about that.'

And then the rumours swirled round the store, all the stories that had been circling around the city over the last few days. Someone said that a black man had raped a white woman, or that a few of them had come together to flay and destroy the flower bed that had the shape and shades of the US flag. 'Bloody traitors,' they muttered. 'Would be bad enough if we weren't at war. But it's just unforgivable at the moment.' Another declared that some white sailor had thrown a black baby into the Detroit River from the edge of the bridge to Belle Island, sweeping up the child from its pram to drown it in deep waters.

Another voice claimed that it was the Appalachian boatmen who were responsible for the entire furore. 'The way they treat these people, you'd think they were still back in the Deep South. Bloody bigots and bullies, every one of them.'

She ignored all their words, recalling how Roddy had decided to go down to the city centre with his friends to see all the boats that either travelled down the river or were anchored in the harbour around there. It was a request he made often; the foundation of his dreams and ambitions to join the Navy as soon as he finished his education in a few years' time. There were one or two men from Hebridean backgrounds who were employed on the boats. They showed him how their engines worked, even allowed him to help out from time to time.

'He's like a lot of people from the islands,' one had said to her. 'It's as if he was born with salt in his veins.'

She shook her head, recalling how he had said he was going down there that morning, how she had acquiesced. 'That's fine,' she'd declared. 'Just make sure you stay safe.'

It was a demand she often made, but one she was aware he would not find easy to obey on a day like today. Head swirling in panic, she turned to Barrington. 'I'll have to go home,' she said.

'Sorry?'

'I'll have to go home,' she repeated.

'But there's an hour or so to go—'

'There might be,' she muttered, aware she had to explain herself. She had worked there for ten years and never acted like this before. 'My son Roddy went downtown today. I have to make sure he's now at home. I don't want him mixed up in all this.'

'He'll be all right,' Barrington reassured her. 'He's a nice, sensible lad. He'll keep out of what's happening.'

'I know, I know. I know he's a nice, sensible lad,' Mairead said, comparing him in her head with her younger son Hugh, who was much more likely to get into trouble. 'But I've got to make sure he's safe. Surely you can understand that. You have children of your own, and you can understand why I have to be certain he's all right.'

Barrington looked at her for a long time before finally relenting. His bald head bowed as he spoke. 'That's fine,' he said. 'You can go.'

She nodded her head, going to obtain her jacket before heading out the door to fetch the bicycle she rode most days to work. She shook a little as she clambered onto it, aware that nerves were troubling her, dark thoughts filling her mind. It was as if the worst possible fate she could imagine was curling into view.

The streets swirled around her that day. She felt herself imprisoned and confined by them, by the walls of every building, the roads and sidewalks, the cars and trucks, even the people whom she saw walking up and down, turning around corners or heading in a straight line along the web of streets that spun out from the centre of the city, spilling into the rest of Michigan and continuing for miles and miles beyond. Even the towers that dominated Detroit seemed to look down on her, their windows cold and sneering as they glinted in the light, reflecting all the frailties and weaknesses she felt she suffered from. It all made her want to stretch out her arms and return to the island from which she had come. Perhaps she could touch down beside the new house her brother had told her he had been starting to build before the war started.

I've put up a wall of concrete blocks, he declared. *At least it's a start.*

For the first time in a while, she felt like moving there – back to a place where all the dangers that existed belonged not to the human world but to one which lay outside mankind's control. The wildness of waves. The brittle nature of rocks on the edge of the ocean. The stretches of bog that your feet could stumble upon as you crossed the moor. Sometimes they could do more damage than that, swallowing up a man and woman in their damp and darkness.

It was different from that here. It was men who did the damage. She had heard all sorts of different people being cursed here over the years, especially during the time of prohibition. The Greek gangs that lived around Monroe Street. The Italian Chester 'Chet' LaMare's East Side Gang with its headquarters in the Venice Club in Hamtramck. The Purple Gang – who were Jewish – which had been responsible for many of the killings in the city. There were even those who hated the Presbyterian Scots, pointing out that many of them were in the Ku Klux Klan, the ones who had lynched black people in the South and even within this city over the past decades. There was someone who had even pointed out to her that the likes of Baby Face Nelson had connections with the islands. 'His real surname is Gillies,' they'd said. 'No doubt where his people came from. And yet they're such a bloody pious bunch. They see themselves as victims all the time and don't realise the suffering they have inflicted on other people.'

She shivered as she turned down the road to her home, hearing the crack of a rifle in the distance, imagining once more that Roddy was caught up in the uproar filling the city streets. She unlocked the door of the house to hear music playing. Not the Gaelic or Scottish songs Finlay sometimes played on the record player they had bought for Christmas a year or two before, but instead the kind of music their neighbour Nathan sometimes called 'the Negro's revenge'. Clarinets and trumpets, guitars, piano and drums. Jazz, she had heard it called, though its melodies and rhythms meant nothing to her. Just a lot of strange and unfamiliar noise.

'Roddy!' she shouted through the noise. 'Roddy! Are you in?'

It took a while to get an answer but eventually one came. 'Mam?'

It wasn't Roddy, but Hugh, her other son. The one who looked much like his father. Same dark hair. Same jutting jaw and nose. Same skilled fingers. Same wildness. She had even caught him filling a glass with her husband's whisky one evening, pouring yet another glassful of water into the bottle to make sure the loss wouldn't be noticed.

'What are you doing here?' she hissed. 'Why aren't you in school?'

Hugh's face paled before he answered. 'A lot of the boys skipped off today. There was hardly any of my friends around.'

'Why?'

'There's something happening in the centre of the city. A lot of the boys took off to see what was going on.'

'And you just came back here?'

'Yes.' He blushed as he confessed this. 'Sorry about that. I didn't think.'

Trembling, she placed her hand on the kitchen table to stop herself stumbling. Tears welled up in her eyes. 'I'm glad you didn't,' she said. 'I'm glad you didn't.'

'Sorry?' He looked bewildered. 'I thought you'd be mad at me.'

'No ... No.' She sat down, continuing to quiver and twitch as she did so. It was as if her nerves had taken control of her body, rocking her in much the same way as storms had done when she travelled on the *Metagama*, her stomach stirring and difficult to control. 'I'm glad you came here. It was the sensible thing to have done.'

Hugh laughed, 'That's the first time you've ever said anything like that to me.'

'Yes, yes. I know that.' She tried to smile in response to his words, but the gesture failed her. Instead, she could see her other son in a street perforated with dozens of angry faces, a forest of eyes and open angry mouths, hands that wielded wooden baseball bats or knives, sweeping them back and forth like the scythes she used to see her neighbours using when she lived on the family croft. And all around the city the acrid stink of fire and smoke spilling out everywhere, concealing the large grey buildings that stood around them, the towers that did not have their windows broken or their roofs set ablaze.

'Roddy …' she muttered. 'Where's Roddy?'

Almost as she spoke, the door opened, and her eldest son stepped into the house.

Twenty-nine

'It's like I said. It's been coming a while,' Nathan declared when the two households gathered in his kitchen and talked about what had happened the previous two days and nights.

Both he and Finlay had been over much of this earlier, pointing out that around thirty people had been killed in the clashes and clamour that had occurred in the streets, many of them victims of the police. More than five hundred had been injured, often black people dragged from streetcars by rampaging whites intent on avenging the supposed rape of a white woman. And then there were the 1,800 or so arrested, dragged along blood-stained sidewalks in front of the smashed and broken windows of stores, cafés, bars and restaurants by pairs of policemen, trying to bring the uproar to an end. It was the federal troops who had managed to do that, being sent to the city to restore its peace.

'The whole thing is a bloody disgrace,' Nathan continued. 'It makes me ashamed of living here.'

And then he began explaining why such an event was inevitable. 'The government, especially FDR and his crowd, have been too soft on blacks over the last while. They're using the war as an excuse for opening too many doors for them. Especially in terms of housing. They're moving in among us – far too close and far too often, these days. The divide between blacks and whites in this city is becoming all too bloody invisible. Posh blacks are moving their homes closer and closer to the houses poor whites have occupied for years. And then firms like Packard's have even chosen some blacks to work alongside us whites on the assembly lines, allowed black women to use the white women's bathrooms. It's as if they think they're the same as us. That there's no difference between us anymore.' He snorted contemptuously. 'They're going to reap a whirlwind if they carry on like that. No damn doubt about that.'

Finlay said nothing for a long while, tapping his whisky glass. There were aspects of Nathan's life he had always kept hidden from Mairead. He knew that there was a Ku Klux Klan gown and robe hidden in a chest of drawers in the house, one that the older man had worn in his former life in the Deep South. He was aware, too, that Nathan had been a member of the Black Legion a few years before, being one of those responsible for attacking a black family that had moved into a house a few streets away. Not only that but he had shown his dislike of Catholics, Orthodox Greeks and Russians, as well as Jews, in their private conversations.

'The only reason I have time for you,' Nathan joked once, 'is that you're a Protestant like myself. One with roots in the north of Europe. Not the south or east. If you were anything else, I would have slammed the door on you long ago.'

Finally, Finlay took a breath and decided to speak. 'It'll all be sorted out, in time. We just have to wait, allow a chance for healing to take place.'

'You're only saying that because you come from an island where everyone's just about the same. Wall-to-wall white people. Wall-to-wall Presbyterians. How can you have a clue what it's like to live in the mix and muddle we exist among in the States? Especially when there's so many different tribes among us. From Jews to Italians and Irish. Greeks and Russians to blacks. Sometimes you have to take a stand against that kind of rabble, Finlay.'

'Perhaps … perhaps. Sometimes, though, you have to allow time for things to settle. Let things cool down and get back to normal. Only then can things turn right again.'

'No. We made two mistakes back in history. The first one was in allowing blacks to become free. The other happened after we gave them freedom. We should have sent them back to Africa then, given them a place to which they could belong. Not hang around cramming our doorsteps forever.'

'I don't think there was any chance of sending them back to Africa. Far too many. Far too expensive for that.'

'Oh, nonsense. It's costing us a lot more than that these days.'

'Possibly.'

And then Mairead spoke, the first time she had ever done so in a discussion between the two men. 'It's also far too unjust,' she said. 'Far too cruel to take people back to a place they haven't lived in for centuries. But you Southerners don't ever think about the likes of that.'

'M-Mairead …' Finlay stammered, his face turning pale.

'Finlay.' She shook her head, rose from her chair and walked towards the kitchen door, racing away from the rest of them in that room, clearly unable to withstand their company a moment longer.

'You all right?' Finlay asked.

'No. No.' She paused in the doorway for a moment, trembling.

'What's the matter?'

She didn't answer.

'Mairead?'

It was Katja she turned towards before she answered. Her cheeks flushed, her throat cracked and mottled, she began to express all the thoughts that she had only revealed to Finlay occasionally for years, spewing them from her mouth.

'I'm sorry, Katja. I can't come to see you anymore. It's not blacks who are responsible for what happened the last few days. It's people like him. They're so full of hate and ignorance. They're to blame for yesterday. When my son could have been killed. They're the ones who are responsible—'

'Mairead ...' Finlay repeated his wife's name once more.

'Mairead!' Nathan interrupted. 'You don't have a clue what you're talking about. You're just a new arrival in these parts. A girl from the islands. Head full of moss and heather. No sense whatsoever.'

'I've a lot more sense than you,' she declared as she headed out the door, slamming it hard behind her.

Thirty

It was the thundering on his door that woke Murdo early one morning. The hammering of fists. The kicking and pummelling of wood. For a moment, he thought it was the sound of a thunderstorm, the clash and flash of lightning. Or even that the war that was coming to an end in Europe had suddenly started to bluster and blast outside the walls of his home. It was such a strange and alien noise to disturb the darkness, one that resembled his regular nightmares. It took quite a few moments for him to hear a woman's voice lacing through the uproar, calling out his name.

'Murdo! Murdo! Murdo!'

It took him even longer to work out who was speaking. At first, he thought it was one of the many elderly women who lived in the village; someone, perhaps, whose relative had passed away in the middle of the night and was calling for his help in the darkness. There were many of them around the place, looking after their parents and siblings, watching them grow old and frail. Moments later, he worked out that it was Dolina's voice.

'Murdo! Murdo! Murdo!'

'For God's sake,' he muttered, tugging on his trousers to cover up the long johns in which he slept every night. He had never in his life expected a moment like this, a woman's voice calling out to him persistently, agony prevalent in every sound and cry.

'Murdo! Murdo! Murdo!'

Yet when he opened the door, he was more alarmed than ever. Dolina was standing there, frail and shaking, trembling in the chill of the early morning. There was another bruise on her face; signs, too, that someone had clasped her neck.

'You all right?'

She shook her head.

'Neil John did this to you?'

This time, she nodded.

'Bastard! What a bastard.'

Thoughts jumbled in his head. He knew he couldn't let her into his house. People would notice if he did that. There would be the twitching of curtains at that moment, the twitching of tongues later. He knew there was a chance that the first part of the ritual was already happening, the rest occurring a short time afterwards. He took the raincoat he wore while working down the croft and put it round her shoulders, steering her from the doorway of his home.

'We'll go and see Tormod and Catriona,' he said. 'They'll look after you.'

'You think so?'

'Yes.'

'Will they even be awake?'

'No doubt about that,' Murdo muttered, conscious that Catriona's prayers could be heard echoing across the village most mornings, calling out for mercy to be given to those who were both her neighbours and relatives. He had even heard both his own name and Dolina's mentioned on one or two occasions. 'They'll have been up ages ago. Only their daughter Rachel will be asleep.'

'I hope so. I hope you're right. I don't want to disturb them.'

'You won't.'

He was correct. Catriona was already standing at the door waiting for them when they arrived there. She ushered Dolina into her home, taking off Murdo's raincoat from the woman's shoulders and folding her arms around her instead.

'You've done the right thing, Murdo. You've done the right thing.'

But even as she said this, Murdo knew there was more to be done. With Tormod by his side, he walked across to Dolina's home in Aird. Someone had to confront Neil John, warning him about the wrong he was doing to his sister, the cruelties he was inflicting on her, perhaps even telling him to calm down his resentment against his brothers in Canada and the States. Murdo knew that there was no point or purpose in getting in touch with the police. Rather than seeing her brother end up in the sheriff court, Dolina would deny that all of his had ever happened, that he had ever lifted a hand against her face.

Part Four

1945–1965

Thirty-one

Mo shùilean togam suas a-chum
nam beann o'n tig mo neart.
On Dia rinn talamh agus nèamh
tha m' fhurtachd uile teachd..

Cha leig dod chois air chor air bith
gun sleamhnaich i gu bràth;
Tamh-neul cha tig sin air an neach
's fear-coimhid ort a ghnàth.

I to the hills will lift mine eyes,
from whence doth come mine aid.
My safety cometh from the Lord,
who heav'n and earth hath made.

Thy foot he'll not let slide, nor will
he slumber that thee keeps.
Behold, he that keeps Israel,
he slumbers not, nor sleeps …

As Murdo stood in the church that day, he quivered, remembering the many times his eyes had been raised over the last few weeks, mainly in astonishment at his own behaviour. He recalled how it had all started; how he and Tormod had gone over to Neil John's house that day to confront him about what had happened. There was the usual shaking of his ash white hair, the wrinkling of his forehead, the puffing of his lips as he sought to deny everything that had happened.

'She's making it all up,' Neil John declared. 'That's her usual thing. If you think she's telling the truth, why don't the two of you report it to the police? They'll quickly see if I'm right or wrong.'

'She doesn't want us to do that,' Tormod said.

'Well, why not? Is it because she thinks they'll discover she's not telling the truth, that every word she is saying is a lie?'

'No. She says that it is her duty to protect the family name, that her father would turn in his grave if she ever did the like of that.'

'Nonsense! She's doing these things to herself and then blaming me for it. Can't you fools see that?'

Murdo did not answer. Instead, he looked around the room. There was a spanner lying on top of one of the fireside chairs. Something she had said that he used to threaten her with from time to time. There was also a cricket bat propped up against the wall. It was something she said her brother had brought back from the war with him, obtained during a short time in a military camp in the south of England. Dolina claimed he also wielded that on occasion, telling her that if she ever took food to Murdo's home again, he would use against her.

'I'll hit you for six,' he declared.

It was then that Neil John came out with a remark he would remember for ages afterwards.

'If you're so keen on protecting her, why don't you ask her to marry you? There's no doubt what her answer would be. She's been thinking of you for years.'

This was what had led him here to the church, waiting for her to arrive by his side. He remembered how it had spun through his head for next few days, a time when Dolina had been given shelter in Tormod's house. He thought of how lonely his exist-ence was, how increasingly he had been spending much of his time standing at the window, watching all that was going on outside. He would catch himself asking questions about where his neighbours were wandering each day: why they were going in the direction of certain houses or crofts; what it was taking them in the direction of the main road that led all the way to either Port of Ness or Stornoway. In all of this, he knew he was becoming uncomfortable with his own company. The memories of his time at war were coming back to him more often. He'd drape the wooden handle of his scythe over his shoulder, carrying it down the croft, and begin to believe he was in possession of a rifle once more, preparing to fire it in the direction of the enemy.

These feelings brought him to Tormod's house a few days later, sitting in Dolina and Catriona's company. He was only too aware that he couldn't raise the matter when Tormod was in the house. From time to time, he had seen him shudder and shake, no doubt thinking once again of the night the *Iolaire* had gone down.

'You know I have nightmares about the war?' Murdo said to the two women.

'Yes.' Dolina nodded.

'A lot of the men in the village suffer from them,' Catriona said. 'That's why I mention them in my prayers every morning.'

'Aye. They're terrible sometimes,' Murdo said. 'They come at me when I least expect them.'

Again, Dolina nodded. 'That's not unusual.'

Catriona bent to lift the poker, scraping at the ashes that circled and stifled the flames. 'Why are you telling us this?' she asked. 'You've never mentioned these things before.'

'Because I was wondering ...' His voice faltered and stumbled.

'Yes?' Catriona raised an eyebrow.

'Because I was wondering ... if you would marry me.'

There was a gasp and giggle. Catriona's hand stilled as she poked the fire. 'You asking me or her?' she asked, smiling.

Murdo blushed in a way he hadn't done since he was a child. 'No. No. No. I'm asking Dolina. It would be good if she moved in with me. We could spend our old age together.'

For a moment or two, there was silence until Dolina spoke once more, clapping her hands in delight. 'Yes. Yes. I can do that. I can do that.'

It was this response that led to him standing here, the words of the 121st psalm swirling around him, waiting for something he had never imagined, his new bride to appear.

Thirty-two

Is e Dia fhèin as buachaill dhomh,
cha bhi mi ann an dìth.
Bheir e fa-near gun laighinn sìos
air cluainean glas' le sìth:

Is fòs ri taobh nan aibhnichean
thèid seachad sìos gu mall,
A ta e ga mo threòrachadh,
gu mìn rèidh anns gach ball.

The Lord's my Shepherd, I'll not want.
he makes me down to lie
in pastures green; he leadeth me
the quiet waters by.

My soul he doth restore again;
and me to walk doth make
within the paths of righteousness,
even for his own Name's sake.

Words that had been familiar to Mairead years before hesitated on her lips as she stood in the pews of the new Presbyterian Free Church that had been built in Curtis Avenue in Livonia. She had rarely heard them since the day she stepped on board the *Metagama*. They had echoed round the pier in Stornoway, sung by those who had gathered there that day, the verses mingling with the speeches that had been made, the sound of the local pipe band, even the occasional yell tumbling from the mouths of relatives who had caught sight of some familiar face on board.

'Best of luck, Donald!' she had heard someone shout from the roof of the building on the pier. 'Hope it all goes well!'

She shuddered at the memory, recalling how it was the beginning of her relationship with Finlay, a time that led to their marriage. They had not been getting on so well over the last few years. He drank too much. All these sessions at St Andrew's Hall and the Masonic Temple having their effect on his health, mood and temper. And then there was his friend-ship with the likes of their old next-door neighbour Nathan, one that had continued even though they had long moved out from there to Lakewood Street on the east side of the city. She recalled how furious Finlay had been with her the day she had finally let slip exactly what she felt about Nathan and his opin-ions; how he had clenched his fists in front of her; how he had slammed doors so hard the walls and windows had shaken.

'The trouble with you is that, in some ways, you've never left the island,' he'd said. 'You still haven't woken up to the fact that this is a different bloody world to the one you left years ago. You think it's the same.'

'Just because I don't think like Nathan ...'

'There's lots of people who think like Nathan! And you've got to have the bloody common sense to know when to keep quiet in front of them. It's a damn fool who opens their mouth when they're in the vicinity!'

For once, she hadn't stayed quiet. It was her turn to become angry and furious with him, mentioning the length of time these days he spent drinking or going to places like the Masonic Temple or St Andrew's Hall. He had laughed when she said this, pointing out that it had been her suggestion to spend time in those buildings when they spoke together in Toronto all those years before.

'That was just to make sure you got a job. I didn't think you'd be still hanging around these places thirty years later.'

'It was because of the friends I made there that I managed to keep a job in the Depression. I didn't have to head for home like so many of our friends from the islands. Even today it's where I make a lot of my connections, get a load of jobs.'

'You're paying a heavy price for it,' she declared.

'Well, damn it! I'm paying an even heavier price than that for living with you and your stupidity. Sometimes it's as if you've never left the island. It's as if you think that life is exactly the same here as there! You've no idea how hard it is to put up with an existence here!'

She slammed the door on him again, only relenting when he had come to their bedroom door a few nights later, his voice low and quiet in the darkness.

'Mairead ... You might be right in wanting to move. A lot of folk are doing so at the moment after the riots downtown. They're frightened it might all kick off again. Some of our fellow islanders are talking about moving to places like Dearborn, away from the city. We might be best to get some cash together and shift too. Somewhere safer and farther from the centre.'

'Away from the likes of Nathan too?'

She heard him sigh before he answered. 'Yes. Away from him as well.'

'That's fine, that's fine. He's as much a part of the problem as any of the blacks. It's the likes of him that's causing many of the troubles in this city.'

'I'm not sure you're right about that.'

'Well, I am.'

She often thought of both their quarrels and conversations when she was in the church in Livonia, listening to people who spoke to her in the language that had been familiar to her in childhood. Some were from Glasgow, Sutherland, Argyll, Skye, North Uist, Gairloch, Lewis. Sometimes they would all spend hours talking about tales from home, like her brother's surprise wedding, one that he had telegrammed her about using the fewest words he could possibly employ:

GETTING MARRIED TOMORROW. WILL LET YOU KNOW MORE LATER.

Yet Murdo failed to do this quickly enough. Instead, she found out what had happened in a letter she received from Ina – how Murdo had married a woman called Dolina, who was a few years younger; how his new wife had been mistreated by her brother Neil John for years, and Murdo had decided to rescue her from this.

People say that he did this mainly to protect her from the way Neil John behaved from time to time. I don't know how much of this is true, but it seems he is a dreadful man.

Mairead crumpled the letter in her fingers, not knowing how to respond to all of this, wondering if there was anything else to the story than what Ina had been told.

But there were other matters to concern herself with each time she went to church in Livonia. Voices whirled and churned all around her as she stood near the door of the building after prayers and psalms had come to an end, speaking about the news that featured in the papers at that time. Some talked about what was happening in places like the Henry Ford factory or Flint, some sixty miles away from the city, where

General Motors belonged. It was a place which Lachie sometimes mentioned when he visited them; how he had been there at the time when the firm had used the police to break up a sit-down strike.

'They used buckshot and rifles and tear-gas against the men who were there. It was the women who saved them. The cops didn't want to shoot them in their backs.'

Others spoke about what was happening in the nation at large, their tongues alive and restless with the headlines they had glimpsed over recent months.

'This whole country has changed since the Wall Street Crash,' said her friend Catriona, who came from the Isle of Harris in the early twenties. 'It used to be a lot friendlier before. Especially to immigrants. Nowadays everyone distrusts one another, keeping their eyes on those who either look or think differently from themselves. You'd think now that the war is over and we're in a time of prosperity, it would be different, but no …' She thought of a lot of people when Catriona said this to her. Her friend's words weren't strictly true. Mairead remembered hearing the voice of Father Coughlin, whose tirades against Jews and Communists had often echoed on the radio from the inside of Nathan's house when she was out in the garden with her sons.

'He may be a Papish priest,' her former neighbour declared, 'but he's right in a lot of things. We should send the Jews back to where they came from, in as many leaky boats as we can find.'

Now there was there the likes of Joseph McCarthy, who wielded a piece of paper in his hand and talked about the enemies within. She noticed Finlay nodding his head when he spoke, arguing about him with Lachie on these occasional days he came round to their house.

'That man is right about the Commies. There's no doubt about that.'

'No. He isn't,' Lachie said, grinning. 'The poor need protection from the actions of the better off. This man is trying to use our fears to deprive us of the likes of that.'

'Nonsense.' Finlay puffed out his chest as he spoke, aware that his own garage was beginning to do well these days, that he had even taken on a few apprentices to help with all the repairs that had to be done. 'It's the opposite that's true. The poor wouldn't get anywhere if the rich and enterprising weren't around to give them a hand up.'

Again, there was a grin on Lachie's face. 'You wouldn't have come out with that a few years ago.'

'I guess not. But then most people learn from experience. Though there's a few exceptions to that rule.'

And then – very, very different in so many ways – there was the likes of Ina, who came down to see Mairead from time to time, her face nowadays like a spider's web full of wrinkles, her hair a mesh of white. She indulged herself in her usual conversations, speaking about what she had discovered about her brother's wedding, the stories she had heard about those who had accompanied them on the *Metagama* or the *Marloch*, which had left Lochboisdale in South Uist about a week before their own vessel had sailed.

'The people from South Uist ended up in a worse place than us. Red Deer, Alberta. Frozen hard over a quarter of the year. Blowing a chill wind much of the rest of the time. We were lucky to escape all that.'

'Some of us had it rough too.'

'No doubt about that. I heard a story about two brothers from the village of Carloway. One was ten years younger than his elder brother. The young fellow worked in the Atlantic convoys for years until his ship, the *Veteran*, went down with everyone on board lost except him. After that, he was posted to Kyle of Lochalsh for a while. Partly to recover from the stress of losing all his friends and fellow seamen. He used to go down to the pier quite often while he was there to see if he recognised any of his pals who were boarding the steamer to go to Stornoway. One day he started chatting to this older Canadian soldier whom he met beside the gangway. They were talking for quite a while before the Canadian mentioned he was going to visit his mother in Carloway. "Oh, who is she?" the younger one asked. It was then the penny dropped: the two of them were brothers. They hadn't even guessed that before. So many changes in their size and shape and colour since they had last seen each other.'

Ina paused for a moment.

'The Canadian fellow also said he sometimes had a rough time over there. He looks so dark that some people think he's an Indian, and he gets abused over this. Once it even happened to him when he was driving across to Alaska, crossing the frozen lakes there. Someone tried to give him a hammering there.'

Mairead's stomach churned when someone spoke about matters like that. It was the aspect of life in Detroit she disliked most; how many people in the city judged others by the colour of their skin or the tone and texture of their voices. It even began to affect her when someone paid her a compliment because of her accent. 'I love your Scottish voice,' they might say. 'It's a wonderful way to speak.' She would shake her head because she wasn't sure that this was the right way to pay a compliment to people, judging them by where they came from rather than who they were. Yet it was the way loads of people behaved here. Even Finlay complained about it sometimes. 'I'm fed up of being called a stupid bloody Jock,' he would declare, ignoring the fact that he all too often judged people in much the same way.

***

Roddy was in the US Navy now. It was not something that surprised Mairead very much. Ever since he was a youngster, the idea of working on a boat had been at the centre of his interests. 'I feel trapped here,' he first confessed when he was in his teens. 'You two were lucky to grow up on an island. Every day the horizon opens up for you there. There's something new in your eyeline with each season. One minute there's a storm. The next there's sunlight. At night there's the brightness of moonlight sparkling on the waves. Here, everything is walled in by streets and skyscrapers. Rows and rows of shops, factories and houses.'

'The shops and factories give people opportunities,' Finlay said, frowning. 'Don't forget that.'

'They can also trap people all their lives.'

'Sometimes islands can do that too,' Mairead declared, thinking of her brother and how he wrote her an occasional letter from their croft, telling her mainly of the people who had died over the past few years, how their lives had been frittered away on their crofts. 'I can hardly remember who most of them are these days,' she had confessed to Ina once. 'Apart from a few neighbours, their faces have blurred together long ago.' She recalled a scolding expression cross her friend's eyes and mouth when she said this, as if she had committed a terrible wrong in this lapse of memory. Mairead returned her gaze once again to her son as this thought slipped away, joining the conversation in her home once again.

'Well, every time I heard you and your friends speak about islands,' Roddy declared, 'it always gave me the chance to dream.'

'For some folk, that dream turned out to be a nightmare,' Finlay muttered. 'People gossiping about each other, no matter what they did. I remember how it was when I was growing up. It hasn't changed much.'

'Some people have said that's a good thing.'

'Really?'

'It was probably a lot easier to avoid temptations here than there.' Roddy smiled, imitating the voice of the minister from Lewis who had just recently begun to preach in Livonia.

'There wasn't quite so much on offer,' Finlay said. 'Most of the people were like one another. They worked the land. Did some fishing. Spoke the same tongue. There wasn't exactly the same variety there. Not of people. Not of jobs. Not of attitudes to life.'

'No. I don't suppose there was.' Roddy shrugged. 'But that doesn't mean I shouldn't go to sea and join the Navy if I want to.'

'True. But I've seen what happened to many men who made that choice during the last two wars. They're not around any longer.'

'That doesn't mean it's going to happen to me. Those kinds of wars are long over.'

'They might be back one day.'

'Oh, I doubt that. Peace never lasts that long.'

Yet despite all their reservations, both Mairead and Finlay finally concluded there was no choice but to give in to Roddy's dreams and ambitions. It was a decision that became real to them on the day a photo of their son arrived at their home from the naval base to which he had gone, one in Norfolk on the coast of northeast Virginia. It was a photograph that showed him in his naval uniform. A white cap on his head, covering most of the fair hair he had inherited from her family. A dark uniform with a neckerchief that was the same shade apart from the three white lines upon it. He looked straight towards them with a smile gleaming on his face, as if he had achieved all his ambitions in life.

'Most of the young people here want to stay in Detroit.' Finlay frowned when he looked at it. 'Trust us to bring up someone who wants to travel elsewhere. He must have inherited our restlessness. I don't know which of the two of us is to blame for that.'

It was very different with Hugh.

He was like his father in a thousand ways. He loved working on car engines, imitating Finlay by sprawling underneath them whenever chance allowed. Even when he was a youngster, he would often be found there, looking at every stretch of steel, checking each bolt and screw by tapping it with his spanner, making certain there was not a fleck of rust to be discovered there. He would ask his father questions about virtually every vehicle they saw passing down the road.

'You ever worked on pick-up trucks?'

'What's that new Chevrolet like? That new Ford?'

Finlay would try his best to answer him, conscious that the day was coming when his son's knowledge would be greater than his own.

'The difference between us is that I was brought up in an area where there were no cars. Only cartwheels. We've had our beginnings in very different kinds of lives.'

'I know, I know,' Hugh would say. 'Your home was a very different kind of place. This one is whizzing far ahead of you.'

It was Hugh's choice of music that showed this most. When he was studying either in school or in his first years in engineering classes at Wayne State University, he would often come home and play jazz records – the likes of Charlie Parker, Thelonious Monk, Dizzy Gillespie, Louis Armstrong – when he either relaxed or studied. The blue notes of a saxophone would echo round the walls of the house, the sound swirling and dipping as if it were winding round the streets of Detroit, trying to find an escape from some of the neighbourhoods where many of the black and poor lived. Or Mairead might hear the beat of drums, the sound growing louder and then coming to an end after, perhaps, it had collided with the many back alleys and walls that cast their shadows on the city, bringing that relentless journey to a sudden, thrashing end. She hated listening to this, wishing that he chose instead the few Scottish records they had bought over the years, an occasional Gaelic song, a strathspey or reel.

'Really? Why do you never listen to the songs I like?' she would complain from time to time.

'Because they don't belong here,' he would argue. 'They're crofting or country songs. They've no place in a city like this.'

She found it hard to argue with him – and not just because of his temper. He might just be right. There was a directness, a simple, straightforward melody about these songs she had known in her youth, much like most of the road that had taken her from her home village in Ness to the town of Stornoway. Only one or two corners. Only one or two places where they had to swirl and turn before they reached their destinations. The city where they now stayed was much more of a labyrinth, with no straightforward direction or journey when you passed through the different neighbourhoods and districts. That only occurred when you were making your way to some other parts of Michigan or Illinois. Even the notes of the birds that surrounded her back at home had been part of the music she had heard there, bringing one or two of the island songs to mind.

Tha smeòrach sa mhadainn chiùin
Binn, binn a' ceilearadh,
Tha smeòrach sa mhadainn chiùin
Ge b' e cò a chluinneadh i …

The thrush in the calm morning
singing sweetly, sweetly.
The thrush in the calm morning
No matter who is listening …

Here, instead, there was the blare of a siren, the blast of a horn, even the clatter of some engine or a yell from a distant street. It would leave her drifting and alone sometimes, caught amid knitting a jersey or scarf to protect those who were in her household, trying with each stitch to create a net that would muffle all the noises that echoed around her. Occasionally some awareness of what was happening in the wider world would slip through. A letter from her brother that told her of the passing of some classmate she could barely recall these days. A note from Ina doing her latest round-up of the news about those on the *Metagama* almost thirty years before. Finlay stumbling home late at night from the Masonic Temple or St Andrew's Hall, having attended some celebration with his friends.

There were other times that were more startling. The envelope crammed with photographs of South Dell she received one day from John Murdo, a man who now lived in Alberta but who travelled back to his home district in the early fifties. Among them were a few pictures of her brother working on his croft, his scythe in his hand as he cut through a field of oats. There was another of him standing with Dolina outside the cramped house he had built just before the war. It offered little room for anyone other than a person living on their own. A 'half-house', he had called it back then, saying that he had left room for it to be extended at some time. It was something he might have to do now that he had married Dolina – not that there was any chance of children. They had left it much too late for that.

Mairead's eyes sparkled with tears as she studied the photo, noting the thin grey hair on his head, the wrinkles that had formed on his face like a pattern of waves emmeshed on his skin by the passing of the years. She trembled as she held it, barely able to see his features in the blur that covered her sight, wondering if the voice she heard from time to time was also beginning to crack and bristle with age. During these moments she fooled herself into pretending she was listening to him, his speech had not altered at all.

'It makes me want so much to see him again,' she declared to her fellow islanders when she met them outside the church. 'I've wanted to ever since his wedding, to find out how he's getting on.'

'Perhaps the chance will come,' Agnes, a woman from Lochs on the island, had told her.

'I don't know about that,' she said. 'I told myself I would never cross the Atlantic on a boat again. Not to go home. Once was quite enough to do the likes of that.'

'You could do it by plane in a few years' time. Things are improving all the time with that too.'

'Oh, no, I don't want to do that either. I can't imagine any-thing more frightening than seeing clouds from above. I wouldn't want to see them that way. Bad enough to view them from down below.'

She knew exactly why she thought that. She had heard stories from Roddy when he had been at home some time before. He had been on the aircraft carrier *Essex* during the Korean War when a damaged plane – a McDonnell F2H Banshee – landed on the flight deck, crashing into aircraft parked there.

'There was this huge boom and blast. It made the whole ship shudder and shake. A blaze started, too, raging over the front of the vessel. Nine people were killed on board. One of them was my friend Davie Goodwin. He had been in Norfolk with me, though he came from just outside New York. He was burnt and died a few days later, after the whole mess had taken place.'

'I hope that won't have a long-term effect on you,' Finlay declared. 'I remember my dad. He never got over what he had seen in the war. And he wasn't alone in that. A lot of men felt that way.'

'I've been all right since,' Roddy said. 'One or two nights without sleep. But I'm okay now. No trouble whatsoever.'

He went onto speak about how the aircraft carrier had been repaired since, helping the UN troops launch attacks around the Yalu River, near the boundary between North Korea and China.

'It was fairly quiet for us there,' he said. 'Nothing really happened. In some ways, it felt more like a bus than a boat. Crammed with passengers.'

He kept quiet about the rest of the places he had been to since he enlisted, conscious that he might let slip to his parents what had happened to him while he was away at sea. Best for them to know very little about what was going on.

'Good, good,' Mairead muttered. 'As long as you keep away from these planes when they land. They're an absolute menace.'

'Oh, I do that. No one is mad enough to run in front of them. Not even me. I'll be okay.'

Mairead laughed at that, smiling at her son. 'Well, you'd better stay that way,' she said.

But then she looked over at Finlay, noting how dark and troubled his expression was. It was as if he was looking back at his own childhood, thinking again of his dad's days at war.

'That might not be up to you,' Finlay declared. 'So many of us have no choice in matters like that.'

Thirty-three

It was Mairead's innocence that troubled him most. Over the last couple of years, he had taken to biting his lip when she talked, especially when she showed what he perceived to be a lack of knowledge about the city in which they both lived. Sometimes, however, he'd let his tongue slip loose, his words and thoughts storm free.

'You've never worked in a car factory. You've never had to deal with the huge numbers and types of people that are in this city. You spent your early years working for some posh folk at Grosse Pointe. Not a black or Greek or Italian living anywhere near there. And now you're at a drugstore. Not many coming in there either. In some ways, it's as if you've never left Lewis. Still among the same kind of people as you came across there. Only difference you notice is that they've got a few extra bucks in their pockets. They've exactly the same shade of skin.'

'Well, I don't know about that.'

'You should look and see the people I've worked alongside. You could tell the damn difference right away. Half of them are mobsters. Loads of them are crooks and thugs.'

She would turn and walk away when he spoke like that to her, her eyes chastening him. Once she even quoted some words from the Bible before she left the room. 'There is neither Jew nor Greek, there is neither slave nor free, there is no male and female, for you are all one in Christ Jesus.' He shook his head at that, pointing out that he had met a few ministers in his time, even in his native Lewis, who had little time for Catholics. 'I've even heard them going on about those from

South Uist who left the Hebrides on the *Marloch* a week or so ahead of us. They never said a kind word about any of them.'

He might go out to work in the garden after moments like that, looking at the life there that would have been alien to him in his childhood. There was the mimosa tree in his backyard. He enjoyed contemplating the fern-like leaves on its branches, the pink-white flowers that sprouted there in summer, adding their own shades to his life. Sometimes their brightness brought to mind the heather that coloured the moor during much of the month of August at home. At the front of the house, there was a beech tree with its gold and yellow leaves, its cross-shaped nuts.

But it was the potatoes that reminded him most of home. He planted them in a few rows behind his house, watching their green shoots appear above the surface of the soil. They were different shades from the ones he had helped to plant when he was young. Russet- or white-skinned, instead of the black potatoes he had known. But he loved to see them. Sometimes he would sit with Lachie behind the house and watch the sun gleam on their lives. He loved speaking with his fellow islander on the days that trade unions or politics were not mentioned. Relaxing after a day working in his garage, he would listen to Lachie talking about his working life; how he had been employed for a short time making deliveries from the salt mine that stretched below part of the city, driving across the Midwest to provide means of defrosting their roads and highways in winter, scattering rock salt on their surfaces.

'It was almost like a secret city in that quarry. There were days I used to stand there and imagine I was still on the shoreline in Point.'

And then there were the times he made deliveries; how driving around the shores of Lake St Clair or Lake Huron was almost like being on Lewis once more, where the sea was always visible.

Or between places like Toledo and Chicago, where he could see the gigantic wheat fields and picture himself lifting a scythe once again and swirling through the long stretches of stalks he could see there.

Thirty-four

Mairead shook her head as she walked away from Finlay, conscious that there was no point in discussing anything with him when he was in one of his dark and angry moods. He would mutter that in some ways she had never left the Minch, that her mind was still back in the islands she had left over thirty years before. There were moments, however, when he was cheerful, when he heard talk of some of the city's black neighbourhoods being cleared for a new freeway.

'About time, about time … It might help clean up the city when that happens. Stop them gathering in these spots.'

Or when Hugh, for instance, obtained work at the new tech centre that GM built near the tank plant Chrysler had constructed five miles from the middle of the city in 1941. Finlay drove out to see it with his friends a few times, acting as if the thirty-eight buildings that stood there had been created or funded by him.

'It's great the work that's going on there,' he declared. 'My son is the middle of it, creating better and more efficient engines for the years ahead. What a pity I might not be around to take advantage.'

And then there was the moment that Roddy got married in Chesapeake, near Norfolk. His bride was a young woman called Lily McDonald, the daughter of a lieutenant who had worked with him for years on the *Essex*. Finlay had danced around the house when he heard the news, acting in a way she had not seen since the early days in St Andrew's Hall. He moved around the kitchen as if he were once again performing the Eightsome Reel or the Canadian Barn Dance.

'She's one of us! She's one of us!' he declared after being told the family had come originally from the coast of Argyll. 'Great to know that.'

For Mairead, it was the sea that was important. She spent an hour walking around a fisherman's wharf that was not far from the town, the sight of the boats bringing to mind the similar kinds of vessels she had seen in her last day on Lewis as she walked with her family around the town of Stornoway. It was not the same kind of work they were doing, dealing with the crabs they had caught not far from the shoreline, but the tang of salt around the quay reminded her again and again of that day, bringing the smack of tears to her eyes, the faint recollection of words to her head.

She could also see a small boy among a group that had gathered nearby, clutching a fishing rod in his fingers. Both of his hands were clenched around it, his knuckles straining white as the fish that had been trapped on its hook flipped and dived, at one moment above the water's surface and then arcing downwards again. The boy's face clenched as he wrestled with it before his catch tugged so hard that he fell upon his backside, sliding on the surface of the stone that was clearly soiled and slippery. Within moments, his catch had torn itself free.

She laughed at this, though it recalled another incident in her childhood when her brother Murdo had been fishing on the rocks near the shoreline of the village. He had toppled too, only saved from falling into the sea by his father's hand stretching out towards him, making sure he was dragged upright again. The older man had laughed loudly after that, the sound of his merriment and amusement greater even than the wash of the waves around the shoreline.

A thousand thoughts came back to mind when she thought about that. She could even recollect how she had told them not to go down to the harbour with her, insisting she could stroll there on her own.

'It'll be hard enough to walk down that street, without watching you by my side. And I don't want any long hugs either. Just a quick hold. I want to stay upright all the way down to the *Metagama*. Not feel my legs rocking below me as I go on my way.'

Her legs rocked once more when she was in the local Presbyterian church, not far from the McDonalds' family home, a few days later. The young bride Lily had two men by her side who wore naval uniforms – Roddy and her father. Her bridal veil swirled like the crest of a wave, especially when she was in the company of the bridesmaids outside the doors of the church, where a strong breeze was blowing. It all brought back to mind her own voyage on the *Metagama*, how the waves had sometimes swept over the decks at times during their journey across the Atlantic, chilling her to the bone. Part of that was still with her. She grasped and squeezed Finlay's arm as he stood alongside her, something she had not done in the last few years. He looked at her with a puzzled expression, wondering what he had done to earn this gesture of affection.

There were other moments she reeled. When her brother and Dolina's telegram was read out, telling the young couple that they could come and visit any time. *The house is open!* It was a contribution to the evening that made Finlay scowl and mutter in her direction. 'None of my family sent anything,' he complained.

Mairead raised a finger to her lips when he said this, aware that he had little reason to complain about their silence. He had rarely contacted them over the decades since they arrived here. 'Not sure I want to have anything much to do with them,' he admitted once.

Another time Mairead shook was when Lily's father, Donald, stood up to welcome Roddy to their family, saying how glad he was that their daughter had married 'one of us', pointing out that his ancestors had come from a village just outside Oban and that his grandfather had been brought up as a Gaelic speaker.

'Something he had in common with a few folks here,' he said, winking in their direction as he spoke. 'And then, of course, he's a Navy man like myself. Something he has in common, too, with a few of the people in his father's family. Isn't that true?'

Mairead watched Finlay sip his whisky and nod in response, not letting slip the hurt he had felt a few moments earlier when the telegrams had been read aloud. 'Certainly ...'

'So, I have to confess that in seeing Lily's choice of Roddy as a husband, I feel as if she's picked someone who has a similar bloodstream to my own. We have a great deal in common. Something that makes both this marriage and his people's family completely and utterly natural to me.' He lifted his glass in his hand. 'I would like to finish by raising a toast to Roddy and his brother, mother and father. It's great to be here with you to celebrate this day.'

Mairead nodded, taking a mouthful of wine, glancing once more in Finlay's direction. She was conscious that he felt much the same as his son's father-in-law: delighted that his offspring had married someone from a household which, he probably imagined, resembled some of those that had surrounded him in his childhood. It was as if, for one moment, he could pretend they had never travelled across the Atlantic; that perhaps they had undertaken the short distance across the Minch to the Scottish mainland instead; allowing him for a moment to deceive himself and imagine that their voyage on the *Metagama* had never, ever taken place.

Thirty-five

There were a thousand reasons why Murdo worked hard on his new home that summer.

There was the money he had received from his own sister, collected both during and after the war. *We know the last few years have been a rough time for you on that side of the Atlantic*, Mairead had written, *but it's been entirely different here. People received a lot of money here in Detroit during the war. Finlay and I have got more than we've ever had before. So, just accept the cash I'm sending you. It will help to improve your life in Lewis.*

There was also the money Dolina received from her brothers in Vancouver and California.

We know exactly why you left the family house. Whatever Neil John says, you were right to do so. We've heard many tales of how he acted towards you when you were at home. And we hope this money helps you to start a new life for you and Murdo.

And then there were the photos Murdo received of Roddy and Lily's wedding day. They were oddly familiar to him. Some of the younger souls in the pictures reminded him of the ones that had left on the *Metagama*. He could recall how he had glimpsed their faces as they gathered round the harbour in Stornoway, for all that so much had changed in the years since. A young queen on the throne instead of the grey-bearded King George who had been in place back then. An old soldier who came from a German family living in the White House. No sign of the likes of either Hitler or Stalin anymore.

It was the photographs of his nephews, however, that prompted him to build a new house, hiring a few locals to help him fashion its walls, put on a tar-splashed roof and a few windows in place. He had already seen how a few locals had returned home from Canada and the States in the thirties, creating new houses on the crofts they had previously deserted. It all went to show him that life was not predictable, that one could not tell when it might swerve or curve, changing direction in ways one could not even begin to foresee. Part of him imagined the likes of Hugh or Roddy walking down the same croft that he had known in his childhood, the path to the shoreline becoming as familiar to the next generation as it was to him.

But it was not only this that motivated him to step towards his new house every day he was not tired and exhausted from working on the croft, a hammer in his hand as he undertook a new task that had to be done. There was also Dolina.

She no longer brought food to his home. Instead, she cooked it on the household stove, laying it on the table each day after he finished his croftwork. He would stretch out his hand towards hers, clasping her fingers in gratitude for all she had done.

'Thank you, Lord,' he'd mutter, 'for bringing you to me.'

Thirty-six

Apart from the garden, there were other ways that their Lakewood Street home reminded Finlay of his past in Lewis. There was that time in June when the hordes of fish-flies whirling through the air recalled the midges that fill the island skies each August, making everyone scratch and itch when they were out on the moor or down by the shoreline. If anything, the fish-flies were worse. They rose in hoards from the banks of Lake St Clair or the Detroit River, having fed on the algae that clustered there. They darkened the streetlights of the areas that lay near these stretches of water, coated the surface of cars, created an impenetrable shadow over the houses before they disappeared and died, blocking sewers when they perished, leaving the stains of their bodies – which looked like miniature version of the lobsters of his youth – smeared on the windows of their home. Finlay muttered and moaned as he hobbled around, grinding their bodies beneath his heels, seeking to clear the mess they left behind.

'We only used to do work like this once a year. When the leaves fell off the trees. Here it's bloody twice ...'

It was while he was doing this that Hugh arrived one day. Beside him in his car was a young, dark-haired girl wearing dark glasses whom they had never seen before. She sat there when Hugh went into the house for some lighter clothing instead of the shirt and ironed trousers he had worn at work that day.

'Who is she?' Mairead asked.

'That's my new girlfriend. She works alongside me at GM.'

'Why don't you invite her in?'

'Well, we haven't got much time.'

'Oh, don't worry about that. We won't keep you back.'

'You sure?'

'Of course.'

Finally, Hugh relented, nodding his head. 'Okay then.'

It was then that Finlay first met Rossella. When she entered the house, he looked at her in a way he had never looked at his daughter-in-law Lily. He examined every detail of her appearance – the tangle of long black hair, the brown eyes, the tanned and tawny skin, the slightly curved lips coloured by red lipstick. There was her immaculately tailored green dress and high heels – the type of clothing he could never imagine any of the girls back on the island wearing at any time, not even on a rare day of sunlight and warmth. Too much drawing attention to herself. Too little modesty. Too many signs of the Mediterranean. Not enough of the North Atlantic.

'Very good to meet you,' she said, her hands gesticulating before she stretched out towards them. 'Hugh has told me all about you.'

Mairead smiled. 'Good things, I hope.'

'Oh, yes. There's no denying that.'

'Good. Good.'

Finlay nodded his head through all of this, a dark stain on his clothes from the fish-flies he had cleared away from all around the house matching the look on his face.

'Do you work with Hugh at GM?' Mairead asked.

'Yes. I'm in the office at GM. I answer the phone. Work on the typewriter.'

'That's good.'

'We see each other a lot there. I type out his reports some-times. Find out the work he's doing.'

'Excellent. How long have you been there?'

'Five years. We've worked together a lot of that time.'

'That's fine too.'

There was silence for a few moments. Finlay continued to glower in the young woman's direction, tapping his fingers on his armrest while his son was upstairs.

'I can't imagine there's a better way of getting to know someone,' Mairead said, 'than by working alongside them.'

'No. We talk together a lot. Hugh sometimes asks me for my help. At other times I ask him for his.'

'That's good. Good. Good.'

Finally, Finlay spoke, his mouth barely moving as he did so. 'Where do your people come from?' he asked.

'From Detroit. Around Gratiot Avenue.'

A tiny light sparked in Finlay's eyes. 'They're Italian, then?'

'Yes. Hugh says that they come from a community that's not unlike the island you come from. North of Italy. They work the land there. Fish a little. The place is full of their relations.'

'Oh?' Finlay frowned once again. 'But what religion are they?'

Rossella took a while before she answered. 'Catholic.'

'Oh.'

At that moment, Hugh entered the room. Looking narrowly at his father, it was quite clear he'd overheard every word the older man had said.

'Dad …' he began.

'I'm sorry,' Finlay declared, 'but I believe every man and woman should stick to their own kind. Nothing else makes sense. Life is difficult enough, even if you do that. Impossible if you don't.'

'Dad …' Hugh started again.

'There's an old Gaelic proverb about that,' Finlay muttered. *'S binn guth an eòin far am beirear e.* Sweet is the song of the bird where he was hatched. You shouldn't choose a foreigner to share your nest with. If the lives of most of my friends has taught me anything.'

'Dad ...'

But he never got the chance to say any more than that. His father turned in the direction of the back door in their kitchen, heading out to the garden, where he knew he would be safe from his son's response. Mairead would restrain him, as she had done so often in his youth, making sure that their neighbours could not hear the bellowing and raging of the two men.

Thirty-seven

From then on, Mairead watched the quarrels between the two men escalate. Hugh said nothing for ages but, for weeks afterwards, there would be the slamming of doors, the raising of voices, even the playing of loud jazz music from his bedroom – Charlie Parker or Dizzy Gillespie drowning out the voices of Archie Grant or Calum Kennedy on the records Murdo had sent to her from home, telling in his letter of how the latter, a young singer from the Isle of Lewis, had won some great award in Moscow. The noise engulfed their home, the shouting and yelling between the two of them.

'You've no right to tell me who I can marry.'

'Don't I? I am your father. You need my respect and consent. Most sons wouldn't dare wed anyone without receiving that!'

'My respect? You haven't had that for years! I've seen the way you treat my mother!'

'How dare you? How bloody dare you?'

'Sometimes you have no choice but to stand up for yourself. You've given me no other option!'

Mairead would cry as she listened to the uproar, shaking with emotion. The noise and outcry reminded her a little of what was going on in the country around that time. A jumble of headlines warring against each other day after day, week after week. Like the killing of the new President Kennedy. What had occurred in Birmingham, Alabama. The riots in Harlem that were strewn all over the newspapers Finlay brought to their home. Even the Walk to Freedom that Martin Luther King had led through their own city centre, making the likes of Finlay agitated and concerned when he heard the chanting, the singing of songs like 'Mine Eyes Hath Seen the Glory', which echoed across the city streets.

'"I have a dream." Hell, let's be honest, I have a bloody nightmare,' Finlay sneered at the time. A day or two after it happened, he turned to Lachie, who was visiting. 'I heard that Walter Reuther and a lot of trade unionists were on it. A damn disgrace.'

Lachie shook his head. 'It was the right thing for him to do.'

'Like hell … All of this talk about people's rights and never about their duties. It's obvious that you've never employed anyone in your whole life.'

In Mairead's mind, there was a sense of life slipping out of control, that what was occurring across the country was beginning to be imitated and copied even within the walls of her own home.

One day she even heard her husband talk about how their lives now resembled the waves they had seen from the deck of the *Metagama*, pitching and rolling and threatening to destroy their entire existence. 'Some days I can even see icebergs looming in front of me, standing in front of my whole existence, threatening to destroy me time after time.'

Sometimes he would turn around and stab his finger in her direction, accusing her of one offence after another.

'And I hope you won't consider going to their wedding, if it ever happens! I hope you won't do that!'

'No, no, I won't do that,' she promised, desperate for peace.

'I hope not! I hope bloody not!'

Mairead said nothing more, conscious even as she denied it that if there was ever a choice between appeasing her husband's rage and going to her son's wedding, there was no doubt what she would do.

Thirty-eight

'*Deus Israel coniungat vos: et ipse sit vobiscum, qui misertus est duobus unicis: et nunc, Domine, fac eos plenius benedicere te …*'

The words washed over her, each sound and syllable as bewildering and unknown as the Italian expressions she overheard from time to time among some members of the congregation, each phrase mingling with the occasional English term she also heard on the lips of some, especially the younger ones. There was nothing about this that was familiar to her. Not the priest in his robes with his back turned towards the congregation. Not the stained glass windows. Not the crucifix on the wall of the church. Not the Latin preaching, which someone had told her was just about to come to an end in Catholic churches across the world. She was used to plain walls, windows that admitted light and not colours. Even a minister who stood within a pulpit that was fashioned from varnished wood preaching to those who sat in long pews. All that stretched out before him in his Sunday sermons were the open pages of the Bible.

She was there on her own. Finlay had refused to even consider going to his son's wedding.

'I don't agree with what he's doing,' he declared again and again. 'People should stick to their own tribe when they get married. And then there's all the children these Italians have. Every one of their houses is crammed with the wee blighters. There isn't enough room for a man to breathe. Life is hard enough without adding all that to the mix.'

It was Roddy who had argued with him. 'I work with people of every faith in the Navy. There's no real difference between them. Good and bad among them all.'

'That doesn't matter,' Finlay had responded. 'People in the Navy don't get married to one another. They don't have children together. Husbands and wives do.'

He glanced at Lily as he said this, noting her swollen body, the fact that she was expecting to give birth in a few months.

'You'll discover the truth of what I am saying in a little while. It's not exactly the same as working alongside someone else. There's a lot more to it than that.'

'*Oratio. Exaudi nos, omnipotens et misericors Deus: ut, quod nostro ministratur officio, tua benedictione potius impleatur. Per Dominum Nostrum Jesum Christum Filium.*'

Again and again, these unknown words and phrases swept over her. It was not as if their own marriage had been an outstanding success. This was even though they came from the same place, shared a similar religion. She felt sometimes that the gulf had been opened between them by the sheer quantity of alcohol that had swirled down his throat over the years, opening a gap that no one could succeed in wading through. Perhaps, too, it was his childhood, the fact that he had lived in a household where quarrels and arguments were a constant of family life. Perhaps it was this experience that had made him turn out the way he'd done.

There were other moments, however, when she blamed herself for the ever-widening space between them. There was something that made it impossible for another human being to have a close relationship with her, an emptiness within herself.

She looked in the direction of her two sons – one the best man at the front of the church; the other getting married to the young lady beside him – and hoped that they had not inherited any of these traits from their father and mother. Perhaps they had been lucky. Unlike them, they had not been raised in a place where there was one tongue, one faith, one way of keeping their families alive, but a variety of choices.

As Ina had told her when she'd shared their family news in a letter, *Don't worry about it. You're not the first exile from Lewis whose children have married a Catholic. Some stepped out of the tribe long ago, a few years after they arrived in these parts.*

She nodded, aware that her friend was telling the truth. She had heard stories of her fellow Gaels marrying all sorts of people. Cree women. Poles. Lithuanians. A Mexican or two. Despite this, she lacked the courage to sit on the front bench, to mingle and mix with young Rossella's family there, conscious that if she did this, her husband would view it as a great betrayal, almost as if she had shed her loyalty to him and given herself to this other household and church. She also decided that – for the very same reason – she could not go to the reception in one of the city's Italian restaurants. Instead, she sat near the back of the building, hearing her son's voice respond when he was asked a question.

'Roderick. *Vis accípere Roderick. Hic præséntem in tuam legítimam uxórem juxta ritum sanctæ matris Ecclésiæ?*'

'*Volo,*' he said.

And then there was Rossella's response to a similar rhythm and pattern of words.

'Rossella. *Vis accípere Rossella. Hic præséntem in tuum legítimum marítum juxta ritum sanctæ matris Ecclésiæ?*'

'*Volo. …*'

After that, the priest's declaration echoed throughout the church. '*Ego conjúngo vos in matrimónium. In nómine Patris, et Fílii, et Spíritus Sancti. Amen.*'

For all that each word baffled her, she knew exactly what he had said.

Thirty-nine

Old Murdo did not need the whisper of the scythe so much these days. There were enough sounds and voices around him in his home. Now that Dolina was living in his house, there were plenty of visitors; people who slipped inside his home to enjoy their conversations and the scones and oatcakes she had set out and prepared. She would prompt their neighbours and friends to eat them, pointing out all her baked food stacked upon the plate.

'Go on … It'll just go stale if you don't.'

There were other things, apart from the welcome they received, that probably made people step through the doorway of his home. His cattle and sheep no longer occupied a barn attached to his new house but lived instead in a separate building. The sheep now settled in his old home, in what had once been his bedroom and sitting room, when it was cold in winter. Their smells no longer filled the air of where he belonged. Now his dog was the only animal he had as a companion, his collie almost a constant presence at his feet even when he walked down the croft to the shore.

Still, there were days when he loved the touch of the scythe's wooden handle in his fingers, the weight of its blade as it swung back and forth in its perpetual, constant rhythm. It was a way – he felt – of remaining fit and strong, of keeping his health when so many around him of a similar age were losing their ability to even step and stride across croft or moor. He would take it out of his barn whenever the weather was dry, using it to cut down the clumps of grass that grew around the walls of his home. Swing low. Swing high. The slicing of each green blade, nettle and dandelion a way of communicating with his surroundings, of showing that he still had a role to play in his croft's existence, of, perhaps, cutting back, too, the onslaught of time on his body.

It was while he was doing this one day that the Free Church missionary, Allan MacTaggart, approached him. His grey hair was all spiked up as if he was one of the dandelions Murdo was trying to crop, ruffled by the wind. He wore the kind of dark suit rarely worn by any of the local crofters, polished black shoes that had hardly ever stepped down the length of a croft.

'You well, Murdo?' he asked.

'Fine. You?'

'The same.' The missionary paused for a moment, his short, tight frame bracing itself for what he had to say. 'I hear your nephew has married a Catholic. What do you think of that?'

Murdo cast a look in his direction. 'I didn't know that. Mairead never told me.'

'Oh, that's strange. I wonder why.'

'Perhaps the letter got lost. It happens from time to time.'

MacTaggart frowned. 'Perhaps she didn't want to tell you.'

'Perhaps.' Murdo lifted his scythe again, turning his head away from his visitor. 'But perhaps, too, it doesn't really matter,' he said.

'What do you mean?'

'Perhaps it's better that he marries a Catholic than put up with the lonely lives some people put up with here.'

'You sure about that?'

'Aye.'

'Well, if that's what you think, I can only feel sorry for you.'

Murdo laughed at the missionary's words. 'Well, if I were in your shoes, I'd feel much more sorry for someone who lived all alone, like the way I did for years, rather than someone who shared their bed with a Catholic. Don't you think so? Isn't that much worse?'

'Oh.' MacTaggart blushed, looking uncomfortable and uneasy. 'No. I don't think that.'

'Well, I do, Mr MacTaggart. Now, if you'll let me carry on …'

'Fine. Fine. Fine.'

Murdo continued in his labours as the missionary walked away, imagining for a moment he was using his scythe to chop MacTaggart down.

Forty

'You don't have to worry about me,' Roddy kept saying each time he either spoke on the phone or when he, Lily and their children, Russell and Carol Ann, came to see them at their house. 'I'm very much safer than most. The Viet Cong and their like rarely attack ships like ours. Too much effort. Too much risk. Most of the time, too, we just stay in the *Yankee Station*, sixty miles or more offshore, sweeping and circling round the Tonkin Gulf as if it were a flaming racetrack, a highway for dragons like our boat. Staying well out of danger there.'

'So, you're saying there's no risk?'

'Of course there's risk,' Roddy said, 'but it's not that great. The worst thing we fear are our own planes. If something goes wrong when they touch down or take off, that could cause a terrible accident. Some lives have been lost that way. More lives than have ever been taken by the enemy.'

Mairead shook as she pictured this in her head, seeing a plane begin its slow descent through the clouds onto her son's aircraft carrier. Sometimes there might be a slight wobble of wings in her thoughts. Maybe a pilot that was too bold and adventurous in his command of that flight, skylarking instead of staying in full control. On other occasions it was the deck of the vessel that trembled, moving because of the force of the wind or waves underneath. In some ways, the thought reminded her of her time on the *Metagama*, how that ship, too, had sometimes reeled from side to side, making it impossible for a person to stand upright or, perhaps, on this occasion, a plane to land upon its deck, the threatening roll of wheels, the loud rhythm of its engine. And then there might be an explosion. A bomb or missile aboard bursting into flame, threatening the lives of the entire crew.

'But we've been lucky since we went there,' Roddy continued. 'We've had no desperate emergencies on board. Most of the time we suffer from boredom rather than fear. Not like those poor souls who are either on land or working on small ships. Life is much rougher for them. Much more dangerous.'

'That's good. That's good news for you.' Finlay nodded. 'Too many of our people have been lost on boats. We wouldn't want that to happen to you.'

Mairead nodded, agreeing with her husband for once. It was as if Roddy and Lily's company was building a bridge between them, one that was needed after Hugh had got married. She sneaked off that day pretending she was going to work in the pharmacy as usual, placing her best clothing inside her shopping bag, telling those she knew to keep their mouths closed about what she had done. They all did it. Even Lachie, when he came round to the house. For all that their visitor knew what she had done, they spoke instead of Jimmy Hoffa and the Teamsters Union, the Seafarers International Union and Hal Banks in Canada.

'You couldn't get a bigger bunch of mobsters than that crowd,' Finlay said, gulping down yet more whisky from his glass. 'A bloody disgrace.'

'Oh, I don't know. The cops in these parts are just as crooked.'

'Hell, no … You've got it utterly wrong there.'

Roddy's return home was very different; his family's presence among them bringing Finlay and her together again. They headed out to the places their sons had loved when they were small boys. Once again, they travelled to Boblo Island, visiting the swan boats, rollercoaster and dodgems that their children had loved in the past. They drove over the bridge to Belle Island where none of them had travelled since the riots that had occurred there near the end of the Second World War. There was also a journey to Windmill Point, an old white lighthouse that formed a landmark not far from their home. She watched Finlay smiling as he walked around it, examining the tower of brick and glass. He brushed his hands against its stonework again and again.

'Reminds me of home,' he kept saying. 'The Butt of Lewis. Even though that looked very different indeed.'

Mairead loved having the family there. Not only for the sake of seeing her son and his own wife and children, but also because of the way Finlay's mood improved when they were there. He drank much less, no longer reaching for one glass of bourbon after another. He didn't spend so much time mumbling at the news on the TV screen, speaking continually about President Johnson, the amount of trouble he felt black people were causing not only in the city but all around the States, in cities like Los Angeles, Chicago, even the Mississippi Delta.

'Nathan was right,' he kept saying. 'We should have sent them home once they put an end to slavery. The world would be a better place if we had done that.'

At other times, it might be other kinds of people who sparked his rage. 'There's too many Greeks and Italians in this city. They should never have allowed them in the door.'

She ignored him on the occasions he acted like this, knitting a jumper or some kind of cap, in the way her mother had done much of the time when the family sat by their fire when they were young. There was a grim, methodical rhythm to her fingers when she did this, as if she hoped that, by the clicking of needles, she could drum out the sound of his voice.

But she didn't have to do that during the fortnight or so the family were in the house. There would be both laughter and quiet conversations then. These took place not only with the children but with Roddy and Lily. The latter was always questioning Mairead about her life on the island. Her father had apparently visited Scotland a few years before when a NATO base had been opened in a place called the Holy Loch on the country's west coast. He had taken the opportunity to go and visit Ballachulish, the village where his family had worked in a slate quarry for years.

'You know there's a famous Gaelic song about the glen there?' he had told both Roddy and Lily. 'I didn't know they spoke the same tongue as your folks did. It really came as a great surprise.'

A moment or two later, Lily took out a sheet of paper and handed it to Finlay. On it, a few words were scribbled.

O nach robh mi thall sa ghleann a' fuireach,
O nach robh mi thall an gleann Bhaile Chaoil,
Nan robh mise thall sa ghleann a' fuireach
Chan fhàgainn e tuilleadh, gleann lurach mo ghaoil …

'How would you translate that?' Lily asked him. 'My father wants to know.'

They laughed as Finlay mumbled his way through the translation.

'Oh, if I were staying in that far glen,
Oh, if I were staying in that thin village's glen,
If I were staying in that far glen,
I would never leave it, the beautiful glen I love …'

'Must be how you think of your home these days,' Lily smiled.

'Oh, I must confess I don't often do that,' Finlay said. 'Apart from a few grim years in the twenties and thirties, I was lucky to come here when I did. I got a steady income after I came here. My own garage where I could employ people. A reasonable way of life. I even got the chance to have a few more drinks and good laughs than I would ever have got at home. Dry as the desert back there. Even if there is a little too much wind and rain.'

He paused for a moment, sipping coffee instead of his usual drink.

'I was even lucky in the way I got here. So easily. One chance alone. Plenty of others got caught as they tried to slip over the border in these parts. Many of them going in the opposite direction from the way blacks travelled on the Underground Railroad, going across the Detroit River to Windsor. Or how these disgusting draft-dodgers travel north these days, sneaking over the Ambassador Bridge or going through Buffalo and the Niagara Falls.'

And, just for a moment, he began to transform himself into a masculine version of Ina, telling stories about those from the islands he knew about, how they had travelled south and north.

'There's one of Mairead's neighbours I've heard about. From South Dell. He came here long before the *Metagama*. Sneaked south to Oregon. Got a job in a store in Portland. After that, he travelled north at the start of the Great War to volunteer to fight for the Royal Canadians. Ended up dead in a trench in Europe, leaving his wife to bring up his son on her own.

'Then there was this fellow from Uist who played his bagpipes a lot of the time we were on board the ship. A way of keeping people's spirits up. The trouble is, he just about exhausted himself and never quite recovered from the voyage.

When he reached Red Deer in Alberta, the place where he was going to work and live, he passed away soon after he arrived. Poor, poor soul.'

Mairead watched Roddy only half-listening to Finlay as he went through the tales of success and failure he had heard over the years. How some had found success when they had arrived in this new continent. How others had turned back home after their life here. How one or two had not even made it to shore on their vessels sailing west, becoming ill or broken as a result of the voyage.

'There was one sailing with us who did not even arrive in Saint John, New Brunswick. I think of him a lot these days. He often comes into my head.'

An hour or two later, Roddy stopped even pretending to listen to his words. Instead, he went out to spend his time with his brother in a café in the city centre.

Forty-one

'Oddly, they sometimes sound as if they come from a place like Ness or Lewis,' Hugh said while he sat there sipping his coffee.

'What do you mean?'

'Rossella's mum and dad say they grew up as kids on the *masseria*. Countryside people. In Puglia, the heel of Italy. A place of small farms and crops. Probably a little different from the oats and potatoes people grow at home. Instead, it's green beans, tomatoes, black grapes, olive trees. A lot hotter and dryer too. Apart from these days, the skies turn purple and there's the clash of thunder. They talk a lot about their lives back home. Even quote from the psalms when they speak about it. That's when they're not crossing themselves and kissing their thumbs when they finish. They do that every time the word God or Jesus crosses their lips.'

'Some of that would surprise Dad. He thinks that none of the Catholics know a word of the psalms.'

'He's wrong there,' Hugh declared. 'Very much so. "For every beast of the forest is mine, the cattle on a thousand hills. I know all the birds of the mountains and the wild beasts of the field are mine."' Hugh coughed as if clearing his throat of the words. 'Psalm 50. Can't remember learning that one in Sunday school. Not sure if it was part of our kirk's repertoire. But her dad keeps mentioning it both in his own dialect and English, a way of recalling life at home. He's even taught me the Lord's Prayer in his home dialect. *Attàne Nèste, ca sta 'ngile, sandificàte jè u nome tuje, venghe à nú u Régne tuje, sèmbe che lla volondà tóje, come 'ngile acchessí 'ndèrre. Annúscece josce u pane nèste de tutte le di, é llívece à nnú …*'

Hugh chuckled as his words came to an end, snarling on his tongue. 'Sorry. I forgot the end of that.'

'It's a bit like me with the Gaelic version these days. *Ar n-Athair a tha air nèamh, Gu naomhaichear d' ainm. Thigeadh do rìoghachd. Dèanar do thoil air an talamh, mar a nìthear air nèamh. Tabhair dhuinn an diugh ar n-aran làitheil ...*' This time it was Roddy's turn to laugh. 'And then I run out of words. Can't recall the next bit at all.'

'You were always better at Gaelic than me. I find it hard to recall a single word.'

'That's because we were very different, the two of us growing up. I was always a child of the water. You were always much more interested in the land.'

'My head whirled around little else.'

'Don't I know it? Wheels. Wheels. Wheels.'

The two men chuckled. Hugh took out his packet of Marlboro and offered his brother a cigarette.

Roddy shook his head. 'No. I decided it was a little risky smoking on board. Seen too many accidents in my time. Lilly doesn't like them too much either.'

'Good for her. You don't mind me?'

'No. Just carry on.'

They paused for a moment, both reflecting on the lives they had chosen for themselves. In Roddy's head, there was a memory of yet another plane-crash on the deck of their carrier. Flames spilling out from it. One of the crew, too, blazing as he ran from the wreckage, screaming as he fell. Hugh thought about his quarrels with his father, the old man's voice flaring, too, around the house where the two of them had stayed for the last years of growing up, the occasional mumble and shuffle when he arrived home drunk in the evening or later at night.

'You agree with the war?' Hugh asked.

Roddy flinched as the question was asked. 'I try not to think about it,' he confessed. 'I'm lucky I chose a water-borne life. It enables me to keep a little distance from all that's happening on land.'

'I can imagine. Not many people here agree with it. Especially among the blacks. Too many of them are sacrificing their sons and brothers for a cause they're not exactly sure they believe in.'

'I guess some of them made that clear. In the Walk to Freedom a few years ago.'

'Aye.' Hugh nodded. 'They're not all that happy sometimes, though I guess they have a few reasons to complain.'

'Perhaps.'

There was a shrug in response, a moment or two of thought.

'What about you? How are you getting on?' Roddy finally asked.

'Oh, I'm fine.'

'And Rossella?'

'She's grand too. You know she's expecting?'

'I heard that from Mam. Good news. Congratulations.'

'Thanks. I'm following in your footsteps.'

Roddy smiled once again at his brother, no longer feeling threatened by his talk about Vietnam. He knew too many people who had been killed in the conflict. Pilots shot down by missiles fired by the Viet Cong. Men he encountered in his occasional visits to Saigon, only then to discover a short time later that they'd been killed in some village farther to the north. There was even one with island connections who had lost his life in some action near Cam Ranh Bay, a port he had visited on many occasions during his working life. Roddy had shown pictures of the place to his dad and a man called Calum, from

Uig in Lewis, who'd been staying in the family house. Their visitor had started to shake when he looked at them, clutching each photo in his hand.

'It's not unlike my home parish,' the old man had said. 'Wee islands. Sands like tiny crescents. Bare hills with rocks like skeletons. It's all a bit like the Mealista area near Mangersta, where I grew up. Takes me right back there.'

And then Roddy had told a story of how he had come across the name Cam Ranh Bay, his voice trembling as he did so.

'I was told some general or other visited the troops there. Told the guys there to "nail the skins" of the enemy to the wall. What a pity it was that a young fellow called Angus Finlayson got nailed not far from there instead. His father was from Benbecula. Lived in Chicago. The shock of his boy being taken … Think it might all have been even worse if he had known Cam Ranh Bay resembled some of the places near where he had grown up.'

Roddy shook away the thought, unwilling once again to think about the years of war he had experienced. He looked once again at his brother.

'What's the place where you live like?'

Hugh winced before replying. 'It's fine. Though it's not as safe as I'd like.'

'What do you mean?'

'Lots of troubled kids in the area. Mostly white. You have to safely lock away things when you're there. Can't turn your back for a moment.'

'Oh, that's not so good.' Roddy frowned, remembering what his mother had said. 'If anything happens, remember to get in touch with Mam. She has told me she would help you out, if you needed it, even give you a place to stay.'

It was a remark that brought a cynical laugh to his brother's lips. 'I can't imagine anything bad enough happening that would tempt me to go home to our dad,' he declared. 'Nothing would pull me back there ever again.'

'You never know.' Roddy shook his head, thinking once again of some things he had seen and heard about in Vietnam. 'Sometimes you can never see what life is going to throw at you.'

Forty-two

Mairead was one of the first people to hear about the trouble occurring that Sunday in the city centre. Barrington had asked her into work that day in July.

'I'm sorry. I know that you don't like working on Sunday. But I've got little choice but to ask. Too many are either ill or on holiday. Can you help?'

'Of course.'

It was because of this that, just a week or two before she was due to retire, she was on the phone to her friend Cheryl in Longs Drug Store in mid-town Detroit asking if they possessed some medicine that a client was wanting.

'Would you be good enough to send some out to us?'

'No problem,' Cheryl answered.

And then there was the smash of windows coming down the phone line, a scream too, that on its own sounded as if it could shatter yet another windowpane. She shivered when she heard it, saying her friend's name. 'Cheryl?'

'There's hell going on outside,' she shouted. 'God knows what's happening.'

'What do you mean?'

'I can't talk just now. There's too much happening.'

Mairead looked across at Barrington the moment she slammed down the phone. 'I think there's something terrible going on.'

Young Barrington stared at her. The son of her former boss, he had inherited his father's balding head, the same intense way of looking at people. He was judging the pale expression of their family's oldest employee, aware had never seen her act this way before. 'Any idea what?'

'No, no, no.' She shook her head. 'But it sounds pretty awful.'

'I hope you're wrong,' he muttered. 'I hope you're wrong.'

'I hope I am too.'

As the day went on, however, it became more and more apparent she was right. A customer came in from the centre of the city, looking flustered and afraid. Her legs shook and faltered as she stood by the till.

'I'm sorry. I'm sorry. I was going to buy this in Longs downtown, but there's hell going on there at the moment. Smashing windows. There's all these people rushing about. Blacks and whites. Fighting and looting. Screaming and shouting. Bottles, sticks and rocks being thrown. Sirens blowing. Tactical Mobile Unit cars crammed with cops.'

'In the centre?'

'Yes. Apparently, it all started when the cops raided a blind pig on 12th Street. Just north of Clairmount, where all these men were drinking till the early morning. That's what started the whole thing.'

'Oh God. Oh God,' Mairead said to herself, imagining rocks and bottles raining down on the city like the fish-flies that swarmed around their home during the previous month, yet much more deadly and persistent, a constant barrage, even more savage and troubling than the way those insects intruded into their lives.

'It's even worse than that,' another customer declared. 'There's flames and smoke everywhere. Sparks gusting across cross-roads and streets. The whole place looks set to burn.'

As if to emphasise his words, Mairead could hear the siren of one of the city's fire engines sounding its horn as it sped past the drugstore. The sound conjured up a thousand memories.

Stories she had read in recent years of riots in Harlem, Chicago, Boston. Reverend MacQueen's sermon, the one he had delivered a few weeks before she left home, talking of how 'the smoke of the country went up as the smoke of a furnace'; how, too, Lot had told his family that they had to 'escape for thy life; look not behind thee, neither stay thou in all the plain, escape to the mountain, lest thou be consumed'. She could see the old man standing in his pulpit, his fingers clutching its wooden edge. There were pictures in her mind, too, that had come into her thoughts the day of the sermon. People's lungs and faces coated with dust and soot. Rats and wild dogs feasting on destruction. Buildings falling and crumbling. Fires spreading as young men overturned cars that had been parked in the city streets – Chevrolets, Pontiacs, Fords – and setting them alight. The stink of petrol and the shouts of joy penetrating each corner of the city as everything went up in flames.

She could recall, too, another day, way back in 1943 when she had experienced similar anxieties to these ones, the time when she feared Roddy might be either downtown or close to Belle Island, when blacks were dragged from streetcars and clawed and hammered by white mobs. Or when these horrors were reciprocated and returned by blacks lashing out at their fellow white citizens. She remembered how fearful she had been, worried that Roddy might become a victim of all that was going on. Or perhaps he might be one of the perpetrators, standing alongside some of his white classmates while they beat up some black man they had encountered near the waterfront.

'Oh, God. Oh God,' she said again.

And then the same words came to her mouth as they had done twenty-four years before.

'I'll have to go home,' she said to young Barrington.

'Sorry?'

'I'll have to go home,' she repeated.

'But there's a few hours to go.'

'There might be,' she muttered, aware she had to explain herself. This wasn't her normal behaviour. She had only acted like this one time before, and then it was in his father's company. 'My son Hugh and his family live close to downtown, out by the Grand Canal. I have to make sure he's safe. I don't want him mixed up in all this.'

'Why don't you call your husband? He could make sure the lad's safe instead.'

She shook her head. There was too much to explain. That her son and his father had barely grunted in one another's direction over the last few years. That if they spoke, they quarrelled. That her husband had been out drinking at the Masonic Temple the previous night. That he had entered the house completely drunk in the early hours of the morning. That he would not be fit to drive today. That if she phoned him, there was only way he would react.

'Let the bloody fool take care of himself. He's there among the Italians. That's his bloody choice.'

But she avoided saying any of this. Instead, she turned in Barrington's direction. 'The sensible thing would be for you to close the store just now. You never know where these fires and tempers might blaze next. Better to be safe than sorry.'

He flinched when she said this, as if he were about to reprimand her for insolence. He changed his mind a moment later, however, once he took into account all the raised voices in the store, the fear and panic so many were clearly displaying.

'You might be right. You might be right. It could be a few days before this is all over, before everything calms down.'

And then, almost as if to punctate his words, they could hear the sound of another siren in the street outside, as if it were beckoning more men into battle, welcoming them to the fury that was now spilling outwards from the heart of the city.

***

Mairead could drive these days. That was one advantage she had over the woman she had been nearly a quarter of a century before, the days when she had cycled to and from work along the streets of Detroit, conscious that any moment she could be knocked off her bike by a car or lorry, or even by the people who sometimes raced across the road from the city's sidewalks.

Yet there were still similarities between that time and now. She still felt imprisoned by the streets that swirled around her, preventing her from travelling in a straight and direct line to her son Hugh's home, the way in which she might have journeyed across the crofts of her native island, stepping down paths that had existed for centuries, crossing streams and bridges. And then there were the towers that looked down upon her, cold as the granite with which they were constructed. There were some which she had regarded as enemies over much of the time she had spent in Detroit. The Masonic Temple in which her husband had drunk for years. The hotels out of which he had sometimes stumbled late at night. However, she disliked them even more on days like this. They seemed to look down at her in a rigid and condescending way, indifferent to all the suffering that was going on all around them. Again, she wished she had never left the island, that she had remained settled in a life that had none of the complexities of the place in which she had spent most of her adult life.

It was all worse than usual today. Even as she made her way towards the Grand Canal, she could see how much had changed in the past hours. A florist shop with a window that jangled with broken glass, stalks and petals strewn along the sidewalk. A troop carrier heading towards the city centre. A smashed refrigerating unit lying by the side of the road, its door swinging open. A helicopter swinging downwards above her head. It all felt a bit surreal. The sight of white kids making their way towards her son's home, clutching a sack or two in their hands. One of them yelled at her, raising his two fingers in her direction.

She stayed in her car, listening to the rumbling of their fists on the car-roof and hood, terrified that they might break the windows. Once they had gone, she went to the small, cramped building where Hugh's family now lived. She hammered on the door, waiting until Rossella opened it, baby Alessandro in her arms, daughter Greta standing by her side.

'You can't stay here,' Mairead said. 'It's not safe. Come and live with us.'

Rossella looked baffled for a moment, her long dark hair a whirlwind around her face, her brown eyes bemused and puzzled. 'Why?' she asked.

'There's trouble in the streets. Riots going on. Buildings set on fire. You can't stay here.'

Mairead's finger jabbed in the direction of the city centre as she said this. She could see the clouds of smoke rising from the streets there, the sky turning orange from the onslaught of flames. She could hear, too, the occasional sound of a rifle, each shot like a drumbeat through the rhythms of the sirens that could also be heard, competing with each other for control of all that was going on downtown.

'Holy Mary,' Rossella gasped, crossing herself in the way that Hugh had described, kissing her thumb as she completed this gesture. 'We're not safe here.'

'No,' Mairead said, glancing down the street where another gang of white kids were swaggering, waving baseball bats that threatened to scythe all that came before them, taking advantage of the chaos that was going on. 'That's why I'm asking you to come along with me. Grab a few things for both you and the kids. You can stay with us for as long as you like.'

The words were barely out of her mouth when she heard a car skidding towards the driveway. A moment later, Hugh stepped out, his face pale and frightened.

'There's hell out there!' he shouted. 'You okay? You all right?'

Forty-three

Finlay was asleep and sprawled on the fireside couch when Mairead, Hugh and the family came in that evening, a half-empty glass of bourbon and set of car keys lying on the table by his side. The television was switched on, but he wasn't even aware of what was on the screen. Some commentator was talking about all that was occurring in downtown Detroit. The newsreels of the day's events included smoke spilling out of stores and houses, broken shop windows, gangs of rioters at street corners throwing stones and bottles at the police. There was even an odd tank rumbling down the road, its steel surface lashed with rocks and glass, the rattle of its wheels punctuated by the sound of bullets.

Yet Finlay was not aware of any of that, slumbering even as Hugh, Rossella and their children made their way into the house carrying packs of their belongings, the children's clothes, washbags, blankets and sheets for the beds in the spare room, a cuddly toy version of Donald Duck that young Greta loved to take everywhere with her. Even the bubble of excitement that slipped from Alessandro's lips did nothing to disturb Finlay. He lay stretched out, grumbling and talking to himself from time to time. Mairead had seen him like this a few times before. Once she had even overheard growling out one of the Gaelic songs a man who had sailed on the *Metagama* was supposed to have written.

Hì rì o rì rì, togaidh sinn fonn
air eilean beag donn a'chuainn ...'
Hi-ri-ho-ro, we'll sing a song
about the little brown island in the sea ...

'Finlay?' she ventured.

There was no response, just another pursing of lips, the twitch of a foot.

'Finlay?'

There was still no response. Not even to the sights or words of the black preacher on the screen, how he was talking, using words that she was aware her husband would object to. 'The sins of the fathers being visited on this city ... Oppression ... Evil ... The price of the discrimination that's been going for years.' Half-listening to this, she felt relieved that Finlay was not awake at this moment. There would be words spat in the direction of the man speaking on the newsreel. Perhaps he would even repeat the opinions he had heard so often on Nathan's lips. 'These guys should have been sent back to Africa when slavery came to an end. They bring nothing but trouble here.'

'Let me speak to him,' Hugh declared. 'I'll get him awake.'

'I'm not sure about that,' Mairead said.

'It's the only way he's going to wake up. The stupid clown.'

Mairead glanced at her son for a moment, aware that he and his father had traits in common. Unlike his older brother, Roddy, there had been times when Hugh had displayed similar bursts of rage, curses and swearing streaming from his mouth.

'Let's get Rossella and the children out of here before you try that. Best that they're upstairs and well out of the way before anything starts.'

Hugh looked doubtfully at her, contemplating her words. It was Rossella who forced him to consider them, turning towards where he was standing. 'Your mother might be right,' she said. 'Let's keep the children out of this.'

He nodded. 'Okay.'

A moment or two later and there was the sound of Rossella and the children going upstairs to the spare room, where Finlay had slept for many years. Mairead heard the rumble of their feet on the steps, the clatter of their voices as Rossella tried to settle them down.

'Well?' Hugh gazed at his mother.

'Fine.'

Hugh stretched out his hand to wake his father. 'Dad?' Nothing. He did it again. 'Dad?'

Finally, one of Finlay's eyes propped open. He looked in his son's direction as if he was frightened and alarmed. 'What the hell?' He leapt to his feet, switching off the television screen as he did so. 'What the hell are you doing here?'

Hugh tried to mumble out an answer, telling his father that there were riots in the streets of the city, that it might not be safe to remain where they lived, that there was the danger of the uproar and trouble stretching out towards their home.

But Mairead interrupted him, her voice snapping away the details of his explanation. 'He's our son,' she said. 'He's got a right to come and stay here! It's a disgrace that we haven't seen either him or our grandchildren for so long.'

Finlay stared at her when she spoke. 'But he's made his choices!' he yelled. 'And he chose Papists and Italians over the likes of us. God help the poor man, but he's got to live with having done the likes of that.'

Hugh stiffened. It was clear that he planned to hit him, but Mairead stood in his way, preventing the swing and onslaught of his fist.

'You're a bloody disgrace, Dad! You're a bloody disgrace!'

For once, Finlay ignored him. Instead, he reached down and lifted both his glass and car-keys, gulping one down and slipping the other into his pocket. 'I'm going out,' he said. 'I don't want to see him or any of the rest of them when I get back.'

'But you can't ...' Mairead shook her head. 'It's dangerous out there tonight!'

'It's dangerous in here. That's why I'm going out.' He went to the door and took his jacket down from its hook. 'Remember,' he said. 'I don't want to see them when I return.'

Forty-four

Finlay was trembling, covered with sweat as he headed out to his Mustang parked in front of the house. He muttered to himself, justifying again and again the decision he had made to turn his back on his son for the rest of his life.

'The bastard wasn't loyal,' he said. 'He turned *his* back on us. And now he's expecting our bloody support and loyalty. No chance of that. No chance of that.'

And he kept thinking, too, of that sermon Mairead often talked about, the one she remembered from a few weeks before she left home, telling of how Lot's wife had been turned into a pillar of salt when she looked back at the home which had been destroyed by God's fury and rage. It was something he had thought about his entire life; how there was no point in existence unless you looked forwards all the time. No purpose or worth in gazing backwards and returning to the family home you had left years before. You had to step onwards constantly, live with your mistakes. Not expect your family to scrub them out just because some of your existence had turned out to be an error. We all had a duty to be independent, not rely on others to help us out when things went wrong.

'There's no bloody doubt about that. No bloody doubt.'

He started the car, a thousand thoughts swirling in his head as he did so. Some of them were about his fellow passengers on the *Metagama*, how some of them had quit Canada or the States to go home because they could not cope with their new lives here. A few of them had even scrounged money from organisations like the Lewis Society in the city to fund their voyage home, never even paying back the cash after they had used it, though they had promised to do so at the time. He had hated them for that. They lacked the strength to put up with their new lives and expected others to make things right for them. And now his own son had turned out just like them. He had married a woman who did not possess the same faith and background, and now he had come back to his family home and expected them to put things right for him.

'No chance. No bloody chance of that.'

He raced out towards the expressway, thinking of places he could go and relax. Perhaps the Masonic Temple or Nathan's house, both locations where he had enjoyed good times in the past. Or maybe St Andrew's Hall, or the different bars that were around there, some of which he had drunk in years before. Or maybe he could go to the lighthouse at Windmill Point, somewhere he had been many times. It reminded him of home, the beam shining from the Butt of Lewis, which he had viewed so often in his youth. A light on the horizon when things seemed dark and forbidding within the house, his father's voice penetrating the walls with his anger.

'What the hell are you up to?'

As he continued to drive, he realised it was a question that could be easily asked of himself. Ahead of him, he began to be aware of the chaos sweeping over the city. The smoke and flames. The medley of rifle-shots and sirens. How block after block of the housing he was passing was darkened. Only a light or two still on. The young lads picking up stones and aiming them in the direction of windows, smashing glass again and again. He was aware of one young man throwing a rock at his car, missing it by a short distance.

'Hell ...'

And then he saw a police barricade in front of one of the city's hospitals; the officers possibly trying to protect the building from any damage or vandalism. He made a wild U-turn, driving at speed to try and avoid crashing into the barrier. Even as he did so, he became aware of something striking the windscreen, a slither of glass flying into his cheek. He gripped the car-wheel tight and tried to keep the vehicle on the road, but even as he tried to do this, his control slipped. The car ran over something in the street and jolted, spinning round and round continually until it struck the side of a truck.

Forty-five

It was impossible for Mairead to know what happened to Finlay that night in July. Was he making his way to either Nathan's home or the Temple, only to crash when he realised there was so much trouble ahead, seeing the flames and smoke, which blurred the view before him? Or was it the effects of all the drink he had consumed that made the vehicle's wheels swerve and curve in the direction of a truck, striking a neighbouring car that had sped alongside him on the freeway? Or perhaps it was that, in his half-asleep, half-drunken condition, he realised he had made a mistake in his reaction to Hugh and his family's arrival; that he should have welcomed them and provided them with shelter and protection instead of threatening to send them from their home?

This was the thought that stayed in her mind when, in the chaos of that hospital the following day with its wards crammed with those who had been maimed and wounded among the clashes and fights that were still occurring throughout much of the city, he reached out to clasp her fingers. It was as if he were looking for mercy and forgiveness for all that he had done in the last years of their lives – a stretch almost as great in its own way as the voyage that the two of them had undertaken on the *Metagama* across the Atlantic to bring them to these shores.

Forty-six

'S e Dia as tèarmann dhuinn gu beachd,
ar spionnadh e 's air treis:
An aimsir carraid agus teinn,
ar cobhair e ro-dheas.

Mar sin ged ghluaist' an talamh trom,
chan adhbhar eagal dhuinn:
Ged thilgeadh fòs na slèibhtean mòr
am buillsgean fairg' is tuinn.

God is our refuge and our strength,
in straits a present aid;
Therefore, although the earth remove,
we will not be afraid.

Though hills amidst the seas be cast;
Though waters roaring make,
And troubled be; yea, though the hills,
by swelling seas do shake.

It had been a long time since these words had echoed round her
head – that day when the *Metagama* left Stornoway harbour,
she had heard a thousand voices booming it out in Gaelic, even
those few people who lived in the town and claimed they did
not know the language mouthing out the sound of each word.
Mairead could even see there were a few who had been near
her that day who were with her again at this moment, their
voices resounding as they joined in the verses of Psalm 46 for
the first time in ages in their native tongue. Some even said this
to her later as they left the church in Livonia that day.

'It's a long time since I joined in a Gaelic psalm,' one declared. 'It took me back for a wee while to where I came from.'

There were a number whom she recognised as having been on the *Metagama* during the eleven days in which they had crossed the Atlantic. There were the likes of Calum and Iain, who had lived in Detroit for years. She recalled how Iain had stood nearby when there had been shouting from the shore-line, someone yelling about how they were travelling to the Promised Land.

'They got that one wrong,' he had declared when they met a few years before. 'This place is as full of problems as anywhere else.'

There was even Kenneth, who had decided to travel to the funeral from his home across the Canadian border. 'I couldn't miss the funeral,' he muttered, barely able to stifle his sobs. 'From our days in Manitoba, Finlay meant so much to me. It's like a huge part of my life is gone.'

In this, he was different from others both Finlay and Mairead had known. Among them was Ina, who had sent her a letter telling her that she was unable to go to the funeral because of all that had happened in Detroit recently. *To be honest, I'm scared of the place*, she admitted. *I don't know how the likes of you can live there any longer.* Mairead had nodded her head and sent her a card a few days later: *Don't worry. I can quite understand that.* It was the same with the telegram that she received from Murdo and Dolina.

Our thoughts are with you. We only wish we could be there with you, especially in these dark times. Love, Murdo + Dolina.

There were enough locals in attendance anyway. They came from all sorts of groups that Mairead and Finlay had come across over the years. Some of the mechanics that he had employed. Some of those she had worked alongside, both in Grosse Pointe and at the drugstore. Her boss Barrington, clearly distressed by the look of her that day. His fellow members of the Lewis Society, who had shaken her hand and told her what a good man he had been. 'He helped a lot of his fellow islanders in this city. He did this quietly, so no one need know anything about it.' There were those, too, that they had come across over the years in St Andrew's Hall, way down in East Congress Street in the city centre. It was a place which people were wary of visiting at the moment. 'Too much going on there,' someone said. 'Not safe to venture to those parts.' And then there were those that Finlay had drunk with in the Masonic Temple. 'We're going to miss him. He was a good man to have around.' She nodded as they grasped her fingers, noting the silver badge pinned to each of their lapels, one she had seen her husband wear from time to time.

And then there were her neighbours, both old and new. There were some she barely knew or recognised, faces she had passed by on her drive to the supermarket or drugstore and perhaps acknowledging their presence with a nod or wave. Among them was Nathan, who stretched out her hand to her, a gesture from which she first recoiled but then surrendered. A shiver ran through her as she clasped his fingers.

'I'm sorry. A terrible event,' he said. 'I know the authorities are saying that forty or so were killed in the riots, but I would say there were more than that. Some like your husband got caught up in the middle of it.'

She barely listened to him, turning instead to those she cared for most. They were all there. Roddy, Lily and their children. Hugh, Rossella and theirs. Other members, too, of both their families, those she had both known and never come across before. They were all by her side when they travelled to the cemetery, watching Finlay's body being lowered into the ground, a passenger in the final voyage he would ever have to undertake.

Forty-seven

'We're on our way back,' Ina kept saying. 'Imagine that! We're on our way back!'

For all her friend's excitement, Mairead barely listened to her that day. There was too much going on in her own head, too many different and – sometimes – difficult thoughts; some related to the day she had left her home island, others to the months before her journey had even taken place.

For instance, it had taken her over forty years to work out Reverend MacQueen had been wrong that last Sunday she had seen him in the pulpit back in her home district of Ness. No one had any right to tell Lot's wife or anyone else not to glance behind her, especially at a time her home and life was being destroyed. Not her husband. Not the group of angels that had apparently arrived in their home. Not, perhaps, even God himself, in circumstances like these. The woman had every right to look back to see the fire and destruction that had been visited on her home and its surroundings, to think of the households and families that had lived around her for so long. A quick glance at those people who had shared part of her life was both human and correct behaviour. Even the bonfires and the gleam of the lighthouse should have held her attention that night they had passed the Butt of Lewis on their voyage. The flames a sign of mourning, love and affection. The lighthouse beam casting its glow occasionally in the direction of both her home and destination, shedding light on both.

She thought of all this and more when the plane on which she was flying touched down at Prestwick Airport, its wheels bumping along for a moment or two on the runway. She was sitting beside Ina at the time, her old friend accompanying her on that long journey home. Ahead of them was a train journey to Glasgow, where they were staying for the night with Ina's relatives.

'They're looking forward to seeing us,' Ina had declared again and again throughout their flight. 'Their father was one of those who went on the *Marloch*. He came home a few years later. Couldn't stand the place anymore. Especially during the Depression. At least there was food at home. You didn't have to beg for it.'

'There were an awful lot like that,' Mairead muttered.

'Aye. I've been sending them letters for years. Telling them how I was getting along. Even encouraging one or two to join us over here. Just for a visit. Just to see what lives are like in the islands these days.'

Mairead smiled, aware that her own story was probably contained in these long liturgies that Ina sent over the Atlantic. With her, she was all too aware that nothing was private. At least when it concerned the lives of others. Never when it related to her own.

She could almost write some of Ina's letters in her head. How, for years, Finlay had drunk too much and too often. How he had lost his life so dramatically. How Hugh had gone out and married an Italian, much to the dismay of his parents. How Roddy was involved in the war in Vietnam, becoming the officer in charge of a vessel there. (*He's done very well,* she would have noted. *Made all of us Leòdhasachs very proud indeed.*) No doubt, too, there would be one or two whispers about her own life too. All the salt and flames that had marked her existence. All the tears and uproar that had marked the last few years, dealing with the likes of Finlay, Hugh and the awful tensions of the city. Once again, the place had earned the words of the motto that some Catholic priest had given it in the early years of the nineteenth century: *Speramus meliora; resurget cineribus.* (We hope for better things; it shall arise from the ashes.) God knows it needed to do so again.

After a day or two in Glasgow, there would be the journey north – on the train to Mallaig and then on the steamer to Kyle of Lochalsh, the port from which the men on the *Iolaire* once sailed. Her brother Murdo had sent a letter to her when he'd found out that she was coming home. *There's a fellow called John Smith from the village who's the captain on the boat. Make sure he knows you're there. He'd be delighted to see you.* As she recalled this, however, she could not help but think about all those who had been affected by that awful experience at the end of the war. The one or two in her village who had been part of the horrors of that day. Her neighbour Tormod, a relative of Finlay's, who had survived the voyage. The others who had perished near the harbour. The men from Port and South Dell and other villages – like John Finlay, Iain Help and Am Patch – who had either survived or helped to save so many of those on board. She had brooded often over the years about how so many of the islanders had been affected by that day, both the salt of the waves and the flames that rose over the sinking boat present on so many occasions in her heart and mind.

The last part of her journey home would be the one that most resembled her time on the *Metagama*. The boat would take her past the headlands and peninsulas of both the Scottish mainland and the other islands of the Outer Hebrides – North Uist, Benbecula, Harris, South Uist, the Shiant Islands; places which they had only glimpsed on their voyage out, and even then, only if they had a telescope in their grip. There would be, too, a multitude of rocks and skerries, dark and jagged stones turned white for a moment by the lash of waves. Perhaps, too, the wind would swirl and shift the *Loch Seaforth* as it crossed the Minch, making some of its passengers reel with sickness in the same way as they had done on the *Metagama* all these years before. There would, however, be differences between that crossing and the one she had experienced all these decades before – the shortness of their voyage this time round, the lack of icebergs encroaching on the vessel's bow, the fact that there was no chance of the entrance to Stornoway Harbour being cloaked and straddled by ice.

And then, too, there would be the faint familiarity of the harbour at which they were arriving. Not like the strangeness of Saint John when they had first arrived at that new and foreign shore. The passport control. The sign of the maple leaf on a poster overhead. The men in strange and unfamiliar uniforms. Instead, there would be the glimpse of the lighthouses she had tried to look away from when she left the island; the dark rocks of the Beasts of Holm breaking above the surface of the waves; the buildings that clustered on the pier; the tower of St Martin's Memorial Church that brought a few dark memories to mind.

But most of all there would be the thoughts that might threaten to overwhelm her as she stepped down the gangway, making her way afterwards to South Dell where her brother Murdo and his wife continued to eke out their days. Going to see their new house and old croft, finding out how the only other member of her family who still existed had shaped and fashioned the narrowness of his life.

Acknowledgements

Many people and books I have encountered over the years have helped to inspire *The Salt and the Flame*, and I am all too aware that I am going to omit a few names of those who assisted me – whether consciously or not – in the creation of this novel. My apologies in advance for this. Firstly, among those I remember, there is my old neighbour Angus Graham, one of those to whom this book is dedicated. When he was young, he told me stories about his former life in Ontario, where he lived for several years before returning home. He also inspired the figure of Murdo in this book. After he had a colostomy at the age of eighty, I often saw him working on his croft with his scythe, an action he undertook again and again. It should be noted, however, that in other ways, his life was not in any way like Murdo's existence. He married his wife, Mary, many years ago in the Free Church in Toronto. Though she came from the village of North Dell, there is no connection between their lives and my fictional creation.

Neither, to the best of my knowledge, is there any record of a suicide taking place on the *Metagama* during the eleven days in which the vessel crossed the Atlantic. This incident was included for a number of reasons, especially to link *The Salt and the Flame* and my previous work, *In a Veil of Mist*.

I also discovered about emigration from the Hebrides very early in my life from family connections, people who lived in the United States but visited our home on a few occasions. These included the late Angus Norman Murray, who eventually settled in Sacramento, California, and the late Margaret Macaulay, whose family lived in Vermont. Another younger relative, George Morrison, who lives in Winnipeg, also assisted me in research.

Leòdhas Macleòd, from Vancouver, was incredibly helpful in this regard. I am extremely grateful for his support. Together with the likes of Museum Nan Eilean, Malcolm Macdonald, Ken Galloway, the members of both Stornoway Historical Society and Commun Eachdraidh Nis and Iain Gordon Macdonald from my native district of Ness, they helped lay the foundations for this work of imagination. Coinneach MacIomhair – or Kenny Maciver – was also incredibly helpful, providing me with many names and contacts during my time in North America. Arthur Cormack was his usual kind and competent self in terms of much of the music mentioned in the book. I am also grateful to Catriona Dunn and Cathlin Macaulay; the latter for giving me her consent to include a verse from her late father Donald Macaulay's impressive work within the pages of this book. I am indebted, too, to Don Macleod who was a few years younger than me when we were both pupils at Cross Primary School several decades ago. Without his tales of his grandfather's life, there would not be a chapter about the township of Trail within *The Salt and the Flame*. Several people from both my native district of Ness and other villages nearby spent some time employed in the smelter located around 10 miles north of the Canadian-United States border. *Tapadh leibh uile!*

I gained greater awareness, too, about these connections from several books I read over the years, outlining the sailing of the *Metagama* from Stornoway Harbour on Saturday 21st April 1923. These included Jim Wilkie's book about the *Metagama*, which was originally published by Mainstream in 1988, and the late Calum Ferguson's *A Life of Soolivan*. Published by Birlinn in 2004, some of it tells of the man's years working on a Canadian farm. Though *The Salt and the Flame* is a work of fiction, I drew on both these works for both inspiration and information.

And then there are the other books I have read both in recent years and in the past which have enlightened me about some of the topics which arise in the pages of *The Salt and the Flame*. Some cover Toronto, others Detroit, while others focus on the United States as a whole. The titles include:

Arc of Justice, Kevin Boyle (Picador, 2004).

The Shattering, Kevin Boyle (W.W. Norton, 2021).

Them, Joyce Carol Oates (Random House, 2000).

The Studs Terkel Reader, Studs Terkel (The New Press, 1997).

The Irishman, Charles Brandt (Hodder and Stoughton, 2009).

Once in a Great City: A Detroit Story, David Maraniss (Simon and Schuster, 2015).

The Penguin History of the USA, Hugh Brogan (Penguin, 2001).

The Last Days of Detroit, Mark Binelli (Vintage, 2014).

Detroit 67: The Year That Changed Soul, Stuart Cosgrove (Polygon, 2015).

The Detroit Riot of 1967, Hubert G. Locke (Wayne State University Press, 2017).

The Korean War, Max Hastings (Pan 2010).

Last Call: The Rise and Fall of Prohibition, Daniel Okrent (Simon and Schuster, 2010).

Vietnam: An Epic History of a Tragic War, Max Hastings (William Collins, 2018).

The Warmth of Other Suns: The Epic Story of America's Great Migration, Isabel Wilkerson (Penguin, 2010).

Imagining Toronto, Amy Lavender Harris (Mansfield Press, 2010).

Fugitive Pieces, Ann Michaels (Bloomsbury, 1996).

In the Skin of a Lion, Michael Ondaatje (Picador, 2017).

There are also individuals in various locations throughout North America that I'd like to thank:

Ripley, Ontario: Hannah Macleod; Dianne Mackay; Ripley Library; the Fig Studio Kitchen.

Toronto: Rob Dunbar (who lives in Edinburgh) for his many recommendations before travelling to the city; Alexander and Kenny MacLeod (sons of one of my favourite Canadian writer, Alistair Macleod); Maureen Jennings; Roland Gulliver and his team at the Toronto International Festival of Authors.

Chicago: Gus Noble; Kay Macleod; Catriona Macleod; Caroline Cracraft, who hosted our book event at the Admiral at the Lake in the city.

Detroit: A huge number of people met and assisted both Liza Mulholland and I during our visit to this city and I will inevitably let slip a few names to whom I owe a debt of gratitude. These include many members of the St Andrew's Society in the city, especially Nancy Waters and Emma Velascro, who have important roles in that society and hosted the book event that took place in the Kilgour Scottish Centre in Troy, Michigan. There was also John Macleod, Peggy Morrison (née Maciver), Cathie Cheslach (née Macaulay) and Angus John Mackenzie, some of whom we met in Detroit and also in Stornoway. Their parents had travelled on the *Metagama* a hundred years ago and all four decided to visit Lewis on the centenary of that occasion.

We found several helpful sources while in Detroit. This included the staff of the St Andrew's Hall and the Walter Reuther Library. It was great to be in contact with them. My thanks to broadcaster Stuart Cosgrove for suggesting that we go to the latter. It was a truly excellent idea.

There are different organisations who assisted in funding with this venture. They include the Saltire Society, which provided me with the Callum MacDonald Memorial Award for my pamphlet *Achanalt*, which I created in collaboration with Hugh Bryden. One of the conditions for this was that I was invited to a book festival. (Hence, Toronto …) I also received an award from Scottish Books International to assist in this. My thanks to Marion Sinclair and Patrick Jamieson for their help in all of this.

There is also MacTV, which decided to create a TV programme about our visit to this part of the States and Canada. Our thanks to Margaret Mary Murray of BBC Alba for taking up that suggestion. We are also grateful to Seamus MacTaggart and his team for their decision to send Magnus Graham along with Liza and me for part of our journey. He was wonderful company, utterly energetic and cheerful.

Several people also deserve my thanks for different reasons. Some sent private messages when they discovered I was writing a novel based on the *Metagama* story. These include those who informed me about both the successes and failures that befell members of their family after they travelled to North America. (One told how one of their connections was linked to the Teamsters Union.) To protect their privacy, I have deliberately fictionalised some of their stories. They are in the pages of this book, but even their place of origin has been altered. One of the strangest coincidences in my writing of this work was when I was approached by my old friend Torquil Maclean in Eden Court Theatre in Inverness. He showed me the Bible which his father had taken with him when travelling to Canada on the *Metagama* a hundred years before. In it, the words relating to the story of Lot's wife had been highlighted on its opening pages.

This was a year after I had chosen to highlight this particular tale in the opening and closing of *The Salt and the Flame*.

And there are more to thank. These include my publisher, Sara Hunt, for her continual patience and encouragement, and my editor, Craig Hillsley, who was once again remarkable in the care and attention he paid to earlier drafts of this novel, pointing the way ahead on a few occasions. Marybell MacIntyre and others provided me with some information and assistance on the voyage of the *Marloch*, which also took place in 1923. Those who accompanied me on my musical tour of the Western Isles also deserve my thanks. Their names are mentioned in the opening pages of this book, but I'll repeat them here: Calum Alex MacMillan, Willie Campbell, Doug Robertson, Steve Bull, Christine and Mireille Hanson, Charlie McKerron, Liza Mulholland and Dolina MacLennan, who were my companions on 'In the Wake of *Metagama*'. *Tapadh leibh uile.*

Finally, there are two people I wish to thank more than any others for their help in all this. First is Liza Mulholland, who travelled with me to Toronto, Detroit and Chicago. She has family connections with both Detroit and Toronto which formed much of the basis for our work together in North America.

And then there is Maggie. Little of this could be done without her love and support.

Donald S Murray

The Author

Donald S Murray grew up in Ness, on the Isle of Lewis, in sight of the headland where bonfires were lit to bid a last farewell to the real-life emigrants who inspired this novel. He is a writer and poet whose first novel – the first of this trilogy, *As the Women Lay Dreaming* – was awarded The Society of Authors' Paul Torday Memorial Prize. His work has been recognised in Scotland's National Book Awards and he is a recipient of the Callum Macdonald Memorial Award. He is one of ten poets selected by Chicago DePaul University for inclusion in the *Poetry East: Scotland* anthology (2023). His play *Sequamur*, which toured Scotland, Belfast, London and Ypres, Belgium, was recently included among the recommended texts for senior pupils in Scottish schools.

Murray's numerous critically acclaimed books bring to life the history and culture of the Scottish islands in fiction, poetry and non-fiction. He has collaborated extensively with other writers, musicians and storytellers and forged connections with artists around the world, especially with Scottish diaspora communities. A former teacher, he also contributes to the *Stornoway Gazette* and appears regularly on both English and Gaelic-language BBC radio and television.

Reading Group Questions

1. What did you take to be the central themes and questions explored by the author in *The Salt and the Flame?*

2. How well did you think the author blended historical events with the fictional characters and incidents in the book?

3. Did you feel more sympathy with Finlay in his desire to embrace the future, or with Mairead's lingering thoughts of 'home' and the family she left behind?

4. In the novel, did you think those who stayed in Lewis experienced a better or worse life than the emigrants who left to start from scratch in North America, and why?

5. Did your parents or grandparents migrate from their country of origin, or have you or your children done so? How did this affect your interpretation of this novel, if so?

6. What do you know of the reasons for large-scale emigration from Scotland's Highlands and Islands during the nineteenth and twentieth centuries? And the Isle of Lewis in particular? Why do you think so many chose Canada and America?

7. In 1938, Franklin D Roosevelt said: "Remember, remember always, that all of us, you and I especially, are descended from immigrants and revolutionists." Soon after the voyage of the *Metagama* in this novel, immigration rules tightened in the United States. Do individual stories of migration influence your view of the issues surrounding this phenomenon?

8. *The Salt and the Flame* is part of a loose trilogy exploring the history of the Isle of Lewis in the twentieth century. Can novels tell the story of a place and its people as effectively as non-fiction? Which do you find more appealing?

As the Women Lay Dreaming

Donald S Murray

A haunting portrait of an island wracked by tragedy

Tormod Morrison was on board HMY *Iolaire* on the terrible night as 2019 dawned, when the ship smashed into rocks and sank: some 200 servicemen drowned on the very last leg of their long journey home from war. For Tormod—a man unlike others, with artistry in his fingertips—the disaster would mark him indelibly. And for the stunned islanders, who had so joyfully anticipated the return of their loved one, no shock could have been greater or more difficult to live with.

Two decades later, Alasdair and Rachel are sent to the windswept Isle of Lewis to live with Tormod in his blackhouse home, a world away from the Glasgow of their earliest years. Their grandfather is kind, but still deeply affected by the *Iolaire* shipwreck and everything he had witnessed.

A deeply moving novel that explores loss and sacrifice, and how a single event can so dramatically impact communities.

WINNER OF THE 2020 PAUL TORDAY MEMORIAL PRIZE

"A book that's big with beauty, poetry and heart … Full of memorable images and singing lines of prose." *Sarah Waters*

A poisoned breeze blows across the waves ...

Operation Cauldron, 1952: Top-secret germ warfare experiments on monkeys and guinea pigs are taking place aboard a vessel moored off the Isle of Lewis. Local villagers Jessie and Duncan encounter strange sights on a deserted beach and suspect the worst. And one government scientist wrestles with his own inner anguish over the testing, even as he believes extreme deterrent weapons are necessary.

When a noxious cloud of plague bacteria is released into the path of a passing trawler from a Lancashire fishing port, disaster threatens. Will a deadly pandemic be inevitable?

A haunting exploration of the appalling costs and fallout of warmongering, Donald S Murray follows his prize-winning first novel with an equally moving exploration of another little-known incident from history – one that almost remained veiled in secrecy forever.

SHORTLISTED FOR THE 2021 HIGHLAND BOOK PRIZE

"A moving portrait of a place and its people ... a quiet, sad but brilliant novel." *The Times,* Book of the Month, historical novels

SS *Metagama* in the St Lawrence River, near Quebec.